This is a work of fiction. Names, characters, places, and incidents either are the products of the author's imagination or are used fictitiously, and any resemblance to actual persons, living or dead, real or mythical, business establishments, events or locales is entirely coincidental. "The Eternity Gambit" and all related indicia are trademarked by Renee Bernard. No portion of this publication may be reproduced by any means without the written permission of the copyright holder except for excerpts for review purposes.

Copyright ©2015 by Renee Bernard. All Rights Reserved.
Cover Art by BMB Designs, Teresa Spreckelmeyer.

No part of this book may be reproduced, scanned or distributed in any printed or electronic form, including information storage and retrieval systems, without written permission from the author, except for the use of brief quotations in a book review. Please do not participate in or encourage piracy of copyrighted materials in violation of the author's rights. Purchase only authorized editions. And feel free to send the author extra money should you enjoy the book beyond its cover price.

Dedication

This book is humbly dedicated to every soul who harbors a fear of revolving doors, is wary of looking silly and who knows without question that they have to earn happiness (and is wrong on that last point because sometimes you just get to be happy because you're loved or because you've realized that it's not a state that must be earned).

It's not the temptations you should avoid, dearest Reader. It's anyone who tells you that you are less than wonderful, that you are less than the original fantastic human being you are (flaws and all). You are the envy of every employee in the Corporation. Don't forget that.

To Geoffrey and My Girls.

And finally, to my Dad. My fearless, funny Dad who would play golf through a hurricane if he thought he could get in one last hole…or if he thought the wind might help his game. I love you, Dad.

Devil May Care

Book Two
The Eternity Gambit Series

∞

RENEE BERNARD

This page intentionally left blank.

EMPLOYEE HANDBOOK

Policies and Procedures
Angel Rules 101:
An Angel cannot coerce or seduce a human being against their will. They cannot lie about their nature. They cannot act contrary to their nature. They cannot interfere or change the course of a human's path without Sanction from Upper Management but must work within their assigned roles and duties.

Demon Rules 101:

Demons aren't born, they're made (or in a few obscure cases, assigned the title when the kingdom they were once worshipped in as gods gets overrun or forgotten). Just like their angelic counterparts, they have a good grasp on the entire range of human emotions/sensations, but do their best not to "go soft" as it's a terrible handicap in their lines of work and in the field.

A Demon cannot control or "inhabit" the soul of a human being. They cannot coerce or seduce a human being against their will but they are masters of manipulation. They cannot instill or create evil thoughts in a person but they can make appealingly naughty suggestions. They cannot act directly against a person without Sanction from Upper Management. They cannot perform any evil act that a human being cannot imagine (which gives them an extremely wide swath to play in.)

Human Rules 101:

There are no rules.

Humans don't generally believe in Angels or Demons and people who say they do are often threatened with medication and padded rooms.

Prologue

"How may I assist you, Lord of Light?" Malcolm asked with the faintest hint of a deferential bow. It was more of an echo of courtesy than an actual display of subservience but he was not pleased at Michael's unannounced visit into Lucifer's penthouse office. The Archangel had used his lofty position to bypass Hades Enterprises' security and simply appeared on the other side of the unoccupied black onyx desk.

Malcolm smiled as Michael's temper bristled instantly at the slight.

"Any word on the new Lucifer?"

"Why, no!" Malcolm made a show of looking surprised. "Now that you ask… No. Not one word."

"It's overdue, isn't it?" Michael crossed his arms impatiently.

"Upper Management has their own timetable, as you know. It has only been a few days."

"When do you expect to hear?"

Malcolm held very still, assessing the moment. Michael's personality was a delicious blend of retired military commander and petulant teenager if pushed too hard. His anxiety was understandable and Malcolm knew it was time to be more diplomatic.

"I cannot say, Lord of Light. There is no protocol for a Demon of the First Plane to make a direct inquiry and corporate directives generally dictate patience. As much as I might want to, I can't pop in to the Head Office and—"

"No, of course not." Michal cut him off then took a deep breath to steady his nerves. "It's just that I'm uneasy knowing that Hell is…currently unsupervised."

"As Acting Regent of Hell, I'm sure I should take offense at that but I can see where you would have trouble."

"There should be balance!" Michael growled.

"I agree. I eagerly await the new appointee."

The last Archangel Lucifer had fallen in love with a mortal woman and recently earned a promotion that spared him the ruling of H.E.LLc. Promotions to the elite freedom of a mortal life were rare in the Gambit and everyone was still buzzing with the implications and wondering what a new Lucifer would bring to the position.

"And in the meantime?"

"In the meantime, we will do our best to carry on." Malcolm straightened his shoulders, a sincere imitation of a soldier reporting to a general. "I can assure you that every employee is making even more of an effort to perform at peak efficiency. We want to prove that we can hold our own but also to be ready to impress and win over the new boss whenever he arrives. Seriously. There's not a demon in Hell that isn't as nervous as you are to see an empty chair behind the onyx desk."

"You don't look nervous, Malcolm."

Malcolm grinned. "It's not in my nature to betray weakness and certainly not with you in the room."

"Good point." Michael's stance relaxed slightly.

"May I offer you refreshments? A glass of scotch?"

Michael shook his head and began to step back. "No, thank you. I should go. I'd hoped you had insight into…"

"My insight cannot match yours. But I have Legions at the ready to pledge their undying loyalty to the new Prince of Darkness and undying loyalty is no small thing when you are immortal."

Michael stopped in his tracks, turning back to focus completely on Malcolm. "Does a demon's loyalty never die? When you lose a Lucifer, doesn't he abdicate and lose that loyalty?"

Malcolm said nothing.

Michael pressed on. "It's not like you're still loyal to Number Three or Number Five? Are you?"

Malcolm was as still as stone, unwilling to speak, but aware of the growing sensation that the conversation had steered them to the edge of a black abyss that stood at their backs.

"Answer me."

It was a command and Malcolm took a slow, deep breath before he replied. "I am under no compulsion to obey you, Angel. You do not rule me and if there has been a recent policy change, I'm not aware of it."

"Screw you."

"It feels odd to even be talking, doesn't it? Just think of it. Two or three centuries ago and this would have been unthinkable, this little exchange." Malcolm smoothed out the line of one of his sleeves. "I think I'm just flattered that you sought me out for advice."

"I didn't seek you out and I don't need your advice on anything!"

"Of course not. May I say, before you go…" Malcolm set his tablet on the desk and folded his hands behind his back. "It is a shame that you yourself cannot apply for the position. You are—so courageous and I think if any angel has the heart for the burden of that desk, it would be you. You are a warrior but you are compassionate when you think no one is looking. What a Lucifer you would have made!"

Michael's eyes widened in horrified shock. "Not funny! You're not even remotely funny!"

Malcolm lowered his head for the first time. "It is a terrible failing. There was no jest. Only regret that I do not see more of you, Lord of Light."

Either he strikes me down into a slick spot on this marble floor or I live to get another cup of espresso.

Malcolm waited and then finally realized that he was alone again. Michael had departed as he'd arrived—without a word of warning.

Malcolm sighed, retrieved his tablet and out of habit spoke aloud to an empty chair. "Coffee it is, then! But let's see if—" His screen changed with an updated memo regarding a new mission about to arrive downstairs and interrupted his speech. "This will be a twist…oh, Hell!"

Chapter One

> *"As this pixilated video from a surveillance camera in the*
> *National Gender Equality Center's main conference room clearly*
> *shows, Senator Robert Mallory not only forgot where he was*
> *when he was inspired to take cell phone pictures of his genitals;*
> *he apparently also forgot that it was his sponsored bill in*
> *Congress last year that called for stricter sentencing of sexual*
> *offenders and limits on internet pornography and the*
> *transmission of sexual images. Ironically, a spokesperson for the*
> *NGEC said that his act might have gone unnoticed since they*
> *normally only use the surveillance cameras for nighttime*
> *security. But fortune wasn't smiling on the man! Thanks to a*
> *glitch in the timing system, there's no denying that this*
> *presidential hopeful will not be making any more speeches about*
> *setting a personal example of self-discipline and family values for*
> *the American public."*

"Wow! That's a classic!" Benjamin leaned forward and with the click of a few keystrokes was able to lift the visual censors to the delight and amusement of every demon standing around his cubicle for the show. "Oh, man! Now, *that* my friends is what I call more than a little embarrassing!"

"Not too much more than a little!"

"That's a tiny bit of embarrassment!" Someone chimed in.

"Who has the self-deluded ego to be proud of *that*? I have pencil erasers that are bigger!"

"Gender inequality might have its poster boy. Has he considered enhancement surgery?"

"It can't get worse for him!"

"Oh, really?" Lillith asked, casually leaning against the desk with a sly smile. "Wait until the press realizes that he also hit 'Send All' and shot that photo to everyone in his cell phone's contact list which I believe includes a few Supreme Court justices, the President of the United States, and his own mother."

"Lilly! Just when I thought you couldn't be more amazing!" Ben sighed happily and the others applauded before noisily returning to their cubicles, eager to share the news story that was about to go viral online and guarantee that Lilly's triumph was complete.

Working in H.E.LLc's Temptations Department had its perks and Lilly was among the top field agents in the elite Take Down Team. When certain human beings caught the attention of Upper Management by setting themselves above others or deceiving the masses, they could be flagged for a Take Down. Whatever secret desire or weakness they had, it was a TDT agent's mission to make sure everything was in place for their fall from grace.

In this case, by everything Hades Enterprises, LLc meant local news crews, incriminating tapes and even a malfunctioning security camera to capture every frame of the fun.

Lilly waited until Ben's cubicle was emptied and then took a seat next to him as he began to work on turning the news story into a very funny music video that was sure to circle the globe before Senator Mallory had his morning coffee.

"It's one of your best! Man, what I wouldn't give to see the look on his staff when they get the latest from their boss!"

Lilly shrugged her shoulders. "I'm sure you're smart enough to commandeer a few web cams to make another montage for the next office party. Of course, I think a better prize would be Mallory's face when he realizes the 'I'll show you mine' pictures he traded his life for will pop up as rainbow pony cartoons from that kid's show."

"And again, I'll just stick with 'Wow!'" Benjamin leaned back in his chair. "I'm going to start a pool to see how much time off with benefits they give you, Lilly."

A low, dark voice interrupted them from the cubicle's opening. "I bet your skins that she'll get no time off."

Lilly stood as Ben nearly fell over backwards from his chair as their supervisor made an unexpected appearance.

Asmodeus smiled. "Ah, it looks like we have a winner!" He held up a file folder for her to dutifully take from his hands, only to pull it back before she could touch it. "Follow me to my office, Lillith. This case will require your full attention and I don't need the distractions of Benjamin remixing a video to a "Blister in the Sun" soundtrack over there."

Lilly nodded and followed her boss but not before shooting Benjamin an encouraging wink. The threat to skin them was highly unlikely but Asmodeus was one of the Ancients and no one in Hades was stupid enough to push it. It never paid to argue with management in the framework of H.E. LLc and when your supervisor had once been worshipped as a Babylonian god until he got demoted into the hierarchy of the Corporation; it was understandable if the guy was grumpy.

Naturally the running Temptations Department joke was that if Asmodeus the demonic Prince of Lust got laid, his mood would improve but no one was brave enough to make the suggestion to his face.

Lilly sauntered into Asmodeus' corner office to stand in front of his desk and wait patiently while he settled in behind his massive desk to activate his screens. His office was a study in mirrors defying any demon who visited there not to get distracted by their own reflection. Lilly felt no such temptation. Every employee of the Corporation had enjoyed superior physical appearances ever since the Labor Negotiations of 1504 A.D. that had tethered them to this plane of existence.

Lilly's visage and form was more pleasing than many in a sea of superficial demonic beauty and she was too confident of her prowess to be diverted by shiny glass. Not in front of management and not when there was clearly something interesting happening. The file folder was opened to reveal a flash of ivory paper with goldleaf engraved letterhead and Lilly's breath caught in her throat.

It's a memo directly from the Corporation's Upper Management.

"You were specifically requested for this take down, Lillith."

"I am honored, Dread Lord."

"We'll see about that!" He pulled his hand across the surface of his desk and one of the windows transformed into a large video display. "Here. Your next target. His name is Jackson Kent."

"Oh, my!" Lilly's eyes widened at the sight, a skilled hunter who'd just caught the scent of her prey. The familiar adrenalin rush reminded her how much she truly enjoyed the chase—but this time, the chase appeared to be an especially appealing one. Demons were a bit spoiled when it came to physical beauty but there was something about the man that was striking and attractive. He had chiseled features and green eyes that bore into her and evoked a flare of heat in her chest. "He is…" Words failed her and a flutter of fear forced her eyes back to Asmodeus. "A standard take down, sir?"

"Let us hope so. The file has been transmitted to your devices but I can tell you that he is a professional athlete, captain of his national championship team and by all reports, a hometown hero."

"May I?" she asked and Asmodeus nodded permission as she retrieved her hand held tablet from her back pocket to scan the data quickly.

Asmodeus smiled. "You will leave immediately for Aspen, Colorado."

Lilly lifted her eyes from the small screen to blink at the announcement. "Aspen, Colorado?" *In frickin' February? Is he serious?*

Demons were not fans of cold weather and the only time that Hell had come close to a general strike was when a rumor had circulated that their office was being relocated to St. Paul, Minnesota. It had been a false alarm but at the mention of any place requiring winter wear, most employees stopped in their tracks and shuddered in horror.

Asmodeus's expression never changed. "Your hearing is not impaired, Lillith. You'll wear a coat."

Damn.

Lilly let out a long slow breath and pushed aside her aversion to snow. "Oh, well. If it were easy, they'd let an angel do it."

The next screen gave a little more information and she drank it in.

"He seems to be low hanging fruit." Lilly ticked off the list. "Single mother, poverty-ridden childhood in public housing where he was undoubtedly bullied because of his racial mix, star athlete since middle school…except…" She shook her head. "No criminal record, graduated summa cum laude on a full boat scholarship, got a record setting professional contract for millions and—" She swiped back, trying to look behind the dry and surprisingly sparse report. "Where's the fire?"

According to the data, he'd spent his money on a luxury condo for his mother and a foundation for children living in high risk environments to create after-school programs, a food bank and a community center in the city he'd grown up in. And then he'd dedicated the rest of his free time to raising money for a new state-of-the-art children's hospital and small medical center to be built in the middle of that same city that would provide free health care to anyone who needed it.

She pressed her lips together.

He's too good to be true. No one, and I mean, no one, is that selfless. It's all a great show of his generosity—which means there's an ocean of darkness he's secretly compensating for and trying to hide.

He was winning championship rings, getting ticker tape parades and he should have been a poster boy for the next reality show on overspending and oversexed idiots.

Speaking of sex...

Her field specialty was men who preferred women, so she had no doubts as to his heterosexuality if she'd been chosen for the assignment but the big question was, where were the women in his life? She assumed it was a long list. Married or not, sports celebrities were notorious for their indiscretions. Again, long experience had taught her that between a competitive drive and a healthy natural overdose of testosterone, athletes were easy marks.

"Not married," she read aloud. "But...where are the girlfriends?"

"His last relationship ended a year ago." Asmodeus pointed at the giant display and the data changed to back up his speech. "It was a woman he dated for four years. By all accounts, they parted friends and she is now happily married to one of his teammates and the mother of infant twin boys."

"Interesting." Lilly tipped her head to one side. "Well, that had to sting a bit. But where's the hook?"

"There's nothing else in the file so my assumption is that it is up to you to find it," Asmodeus said. "Improvisation is supposed to be your strong suit, Lillith."

Lilly looked back and forth from the device in her hand and the giant display that still revealed Jackson Kent's face. The rest was a mystery. No notes on drug use, gambling, or a weakness for paid sex. Even his credit report was ridiculously pristine. But the file seemed incomplete and that, in and of itself, was odd.

Beyond odd.

But there had to be something he was hiding.

To get flagged for a Corporate sanctioned Take Down, there was always something. Human beings in the path of the Temptations Department were not there by random chance or bad luck. Upper Management alone had the power to set missions in motion and demons took a great deal of pleasure in knowing that no matter how twisted the game plan, they were inadvertently acting at the behest of the good guys.

She ran an online scan for the usual trends or sinful secrets that would betray the monster behind the mask. "Into little girls? Dog fighting? Pictures of pain?" she whispered but the search came up empty. *Rats!*

"Problem?" Asmodeus's tone sent an icy jolt of disgust through her system and she immediately realized she'd forgotten she was in his presence. She squared her shoulders to face him, her expression calm.

"No, sir."

"Find his weakness, orchestrate his destruction and get out. It's a charity event over the weekend. Arrangements have been made and you are to leave within three hours. We are on a deadline with this one, Lillith. Finish it before the fundraising event is over."

She lifted her chin a fraction of an inch. "I'll be back in the office by Monday with his balls in a bag."

Asmodeus smiled humorlessly. "Don't botch this one, Lilly. I don't like the way it smells so take him down, fast and hard, and by the book."

"Have I ever failed you, sir?" she asked.

"There is always a first time, Temptress." Asmodeus waved his arm in dismissal and the displays returned to mirrors.

She retreated without turning her back until she'd stepped through his doorway and pivoted to hurry to her sleeping quarters. *Three hours to prep and pack. Oh, and catch a quick shower!*

Mallory had never completely achieved her but she had her own rituals when it came to scraping the stench of a take down from her skin before attempting the next one. A demonic Temptress of the First Plane had standards, after all!

Chapter Two

Jackson Kent was doing his best to focus on the phone and texts in his hand and not necessarily on the grating chatter of the hotel's concierge at his elbow. He'd just arrived and was wishing that his assistant were there to run interference for him. But Mark had come down with the mother of all flus in the middle of the night last night and was still in L.A. His calls were extremely pitiful and made Jackson smile.

Is it me or is he mixing me up with one of his previous clients? He's sent in a backup but it's not like I can't tie my own shoes for a weekend, for God's sake. Although, I do love the way Mark clears a path when I'm on a tight schedule…

"I'm sure you'll find everything in order for your gala event this weekend, Mr. Kent. We've been working hard with your coordinator, Ms. Marsh, but of course, we're just honored that you'd choose the historic Birchwood Grand Hotel for the occasion. Aspen, Colorado is no stranger to luxury but the Birchwood sets a—"

An odd grinding and banging sound cut the man off and Jackson looked up to see the source of the commotion that might rescue him from the life-size hotel brochure's speech—and nearly dropped his cell phone.

A woman, juggling luggage, an oversized purse and a pair of loose skis, had lost the battle and the skis had wedged into the automated revolving doors, trapping her in what could only be described as a dangerous and humiliating carousel ride.

Someone in the lobby started laughing while other bystanders started firing up their phones to be sure to capture internet video gold.

Jackson launched into action.

It was all a blur and there wasn't a lot of strategy involved in his rescue effort. An electronic alarm sounded somewhere but he wasn't listening. Pride was the first sacrifice he made as the door caught him in the chest with bruising force as he pushed himself against it to slow the merciless turn of the revolving wheel, and then he stopped paying attention.

Because she looked up at him through the glass partition, distress and embarrassment instantly telegraphing from eyes the color of pure jade spiked with gold and Jackson felt like a man struck by lightning. Pretty women were a common occurrence in the world he lived in and Jackson had never hidden the fact that he loved the view.

But this was a vista he'd never seen.

Oh. Wow. I think my brain just shut off.

She parted her lips as if to speak and Jackson verified that his malfunction was official. Whatever else was happening, logic abandoned him as his senses took a quick inventory of the goddess-like beauty trapped in the hotel's version of a giant glass blender. Pale cheeks flushed with pink, a mouth so ripe it made him want to howl, and balanced curves without a single sharp edge.

Jackson had to bite the inside of his cheek to keep his jaw from dropping.

She was lush and impossibly beautiful; and Jackson would have probably said something stupid along those lines if the sound of something snapping didn't pull him back with a vicious yank to the present problem.

"What was that?" he asked, anxious to hear that he hadn't just heard one of her bones breaking.

"I think one of my skis just died the death," she answered, her voice muffled by the glass between them.

Shouts from the hotel staff were audible and Jackson watched in relief as the doorman finally hit the red emergency stop button and the machine froze.

Of course, she's still in there, but at least the blender's off. Man, what a way to meet the woman of your dreams!

"Are you all right, Mr. Kent?" the concierge asked.

"Never mind me!" He had to count to three to keep from really barking at the man. Jackson turned to look back at her and tried his best all in a day's work grin. "I think we can just push it manually and get you out of there, okay?"

She eyed the ski that was wedged horizontally at waist height between the inner wall and the outer curved enclosure. "If you say so."

"I got you!" Jackson said calmly, planting his foot against one of the glass walls and pushing, as several of the hotel staff now joined in the effort. Within seconds, she was free and finally inside the hotel along with most of her belongings.

She ran a trembling hand through dark auburn hair. "So much for a graceful entrance!"

"Are you hurt?" he asked.

She smiled. "You mean, besides my ego?"

The manager approached at a run. "It's impossible! I'm Mr. Yarborough, the General Manager of the Birchwood. The safety's set to stop the revolving doors the second they encounter any resistance! I am so sorry, miss! And of course, my thanks to you, sir, for saving the day and preventing—"

Jackson held up a hand. "No thanks necessary! But I'd say you owe the lady more than a verbal apology. A pair of skis, at the very least, wouldn't you say?"

"Oh, please, don't make a fuss!" she said. "Stupid not to have a case for them but—that's what I get for rushing out the door to get here. Oh, well. I'm not...much of a skier to begin with, so it's not actually a great loss. I should probably thank you for saving me the...embarrassment of sliding down the mountain on my ass."

Her eyes widened in miserable shock as the last word slipped past her lips and Jackson was entranced as his newly discovered goddess looked like a woman about to burst into tears at the simple trespass.

"I'm—sorry," she apologized. "It's been...quite a morning."

"Well," the manager said as he straightened his jacket. "I will speak to the outside staff to see how it was even possible for a guest to walk past them with their luggage and gear without a single offer of assistance. And on behalf of the Birchwood Grand Hotel, I offer my sincere apologies for the incident." He signaled a bellboy and turned his attention to Jackson. "Allow me to assure you, Mr. Kent, that the rest of your weekend will go flawlessly and that this bizarre aberration does not reflect the level of service you and your guests can expect."

She'd started to assist the bellboy with her things as the man rattled on but Jackson ignored him and began to lift her luggage onto the cart.

"Here, I'll get that."

"Please don't, Mr. Kent."

"You know who I am?" he asked with a smile, feigning surprise that she'd recognized him. Celebrity may have its drawbacks but it also had its perks and he was happy if his fame might earn him a few points with her.

She dropped her mangled skis onto the pile. "Didn't the manager just call you Mr. Kent? Or was that a—" Her eyes widened. "Oh. You're Jackson Kent."

"The one and only."

Her reaction was not what he was hoping for. The blush she'd been fighting off in the entryway blazed back into life and she took a full step back. "Of course you are. If you'll excuse me," she said. "I'm just...going to check in."

She turned and walked away, head held high and left him standing speechless.

He started to follow her, his impulse to catch up to her and beg her forgiveness for being Jackson Kent and maybe offering to be John Doe or Dr. Pepper if it would allow him to get her name and buy her a drink.

The manager unknowingly stopped him as he moved into Jackson's sightlines. "It's impossible, sir!"

"Pardon?" Jackson did his best to give the man his attention. "What's impossible?"

"I meant what I said. The door has been safety tested to exacting standards and there is no reason for that motor not to have shut down. If she'd pressed for monetary compensation, I wouldn't have been surprised, sir. It's a common ruse to make a huge ruckus on the doorstep of a—"

Jackson's anger was total. "You're not accusing that woman of some sort of con, are you?"

Yarborough stiffened. "Not directly, but there are no less than four men on duty outside, not including Jefferson, the doorman. In sixteen years that I've had the helm, no one has ever gotten out of a vehicle without being helped out of their car; much less, been ignored to haul their luggage or loose skis into—"

"There's always a first time, Mr. Yarborough." Jackson crossed his arms and ignored the vibration of his phone in his jacket pocket. "But let's ease your conscience. Please upgrade her to the best suite you've got available and you put every penny of her room and expenses on my tab. If it's a con, then I'll take the hit. And let's keep your theories and accusations to a minimum unless you've got proof, sir. Because I don't see how she "made" your door go haywire, even if she did sail past your crew and commit the crime of not asking for help with the bags. She could have been seriously injured and while she wasn't, she was certainly terrified." He leaned in, quietly asserting himself. "And let's not forget, I experienced first hand how hard that thing was turning when it nearly broke my collarbone, so that wasn't theatrics on her part."

"Yes, sir. And the Birchwood is pleased to absorb her bill and see that she has an executive suite for her difficulties. There's no need for you to make such a gallant gesture." The manager began to retreat. "I'll see to it personally and again, we're so glad to have you here, Mr. Kent."

He scurried off before Jackson could gain any more steam.

Shaking it off, Jackson headed toward registration to see if he could catch his mystery girl and make a better pitch for that drink. But by the time he'd crossed the vast lobby, there was no sign of her.

Anywhere.

Jackson scanned the lobby, unsure of how she could have disappeared without a trace. He growled in frustration. The fundraising weekend was a huge undertaking and he didn't have a lot of free time to divert from his schedule, but… *Oh, well. It's a good size hotel so maybe I can find her again. Or get the front desk to give her a message.*

His phone buzzed again insistently and Jackson reluctantly took Marsh's call. "Here."

"Are you in? Mark asked me to ensure that nothing went wrong and I thought you texted that you'd arrived but that was ten minutes ago." Miss Laurel Marsh wasn't the kind of woman who wasted time on small talk. There would be no "how was your flight?" He was late and from her tone, he could tell she was wondering if he was incapable of finding the elevators.

"I'm here in the lobby. Just taking it in." Jackson looked back across the lobby hoping for a break, but his dream girl was still MIA.

"The stylist is here and we need to get you ready for the opening event tonight."

"It's hours away." As he talked, Jackson circled back to the seating areas to see if she might be perched in one of the oversized chairs out of sight. "And it's not like I'm performing a big musical number, Laurel. It's a giant cocktail party for our biggest contributors. I think I can hold a drink and make conversation without having to get a makeover."

"Mr. Kent. Time flies and we need to tuck you away a bit before your big entrance this evening. People have paid good money to attend and for the opportunity to meet you, so it doesn't help if you're strolling around the lobby giving it up for free."

He rolled his eyes. "Did you mean to make me sound like a hooker?"

Even her laugh was crisp and business-like. "We're doing this for the children remember? I'm the best at what I do, Mr. Kent, and I'm telling you that if you dilute the product, we won't meet our fund-raising goals, will we?"

Product. God, I hate it when someone calls me that.

"I'll be upstairs in a few minutes." He hung up on her before she could say anything else, furious at himself for being so smug and messing up what might have been the chance of a lifetime. "Damn it," he muttered to himself. "The one and only Jackson Kent? More like the one and only jerk who forgot to get her name."

Lillith tipped the bellman after instructing him to simply dump her stuff in the middle of the floor. She leaned against the hotel room door and bolted it, pressing her forehead against the evacuation plan posted next to the peephole.

Seduction is supposed to be eighty percent planning and twenty percent improvisation! Not the other way around!

She groaned at the bungled opening she'd made. "Stupid skis! I hate snow! Why couldn't the man have the decency to have an event in the Caribbean like any other rich philanthropist?" Lillith closed her eyes. The worst of it was that the Temptation Department's mission executions were infamously flawless, so the foul-up would immediately be blamed on her—no matter how much she waved around the report that indicated the lobby would be clear and that his first appearance would be at the cocktail party opener that evening. Not to mention the prop department that had slyly handed her loose skis two seconds before transport…

A demonic field agent was supposed to be without equal for their professionalism and focus on the prize. They were most definitely not supposed to make an ass out of themselves in front of a hundred and four human witnesses, including their quarry, and then top it off by snapping a pair of three thousand dollar skis.

That expense report is going to be a bitch to turn in…

She shifted around to open her eyes, take a few cleansing breaths and regroup. She lifted her phone and fired off a scathing text to Benjamin to tell him that they needed to check their image files because apparently her target's photo in the report was so far off it was laughable.

I know good-looking and that—that man was… That man was demonically handsome!

She replayed the meeting in her mind and decided to accentuate the positives. She'd improvised in the moment and made the choice to play the ingénue, softening her approach to match the blazing color in her cheeks. He'd scrambled the script she'd composed in her head.

Well, between that frickin' revolving door and Captain America's smile, I'd say getting a single intelligible word out is going to go in the win column, damn it!

"I definitely made a memorable first impression. I caught his eye. And," she pushed away from the door and headed for her luggage, "that's always the first step. Let's pretend we orchestrated that cute-meet and keep moving, woman."

I'll just make sure his second look makes him forget everything else.

She vigorously set the skis upright in the garbage can in the corner by the desk and then made quick work of unpacking to set up the creature comforts she preferred. Lillith began to prepare for the battle ahead. Her initial strategy to "be aggressively sexual" was scrapped. He'd responded well to her as a damsel in distress and only she would know how ridiculous that scene had really been. Her withdrawal had been the only stroke of genius she'd managed. It was a good opening gambit that had left him wanting more and added a touch of mystery to the encounter.

Now she'd regain ground by gliding into that party sans skis and see if he took the bait. She'd packed enough clothes for a week. Lillith ran her hands over some of the sumptuous and sexy choices she'd made, sighing with regret that she would never to get to wear a fraction of them. After all, Jackson Kent was little better than a jock and odds were she'd have his pants off before midnight and that would be that. Although the trick wasn't in getting a man to drop his pants, the *real* trick was in finding out where he was weak, why Upper Management wanted him exposed and how to make sure it happened in a gloriously embarrassing public explosion. She fingered the indulgence of the fur wrap she'd smuggled into the requisition lists and then smiled.

May as well have as much fun as I can while I can!

Lilly retrieved her perfume and set it on vanity to admire the shimmering gold liquid inside. A temptress's scent was unique to each agent and one of her most potent weapons. She caressed the cut crystal and smiled. A human perfume maker would sell their souls for a fraction of an ounce of it if they caught a whiff and more than one well-heeled nobleman in centuries past had dropped to his knees from its effects. She sighed. Everything in her make-up case packed a little extra punch thanks to the technicians in Hades Enterprises. Not as a crutch but from her perspective, it never hurt to bring a little demonic magic to the table.

Lilly lifted a beaded cocktail dress covered with black bugle beads that shimmered and shimmied with every move she made. She loved the cool glass weight of it and the fit. It would highlight her figure shamelessly and make her feel ruthlessly sexy.

"You'll be lucky to make it to midnight after you get an eyeful of me in this, big boy." She hung the dress in the closet and began to put everything away while she ran a large bath. The indulgence would give her time to refocus, relax and compose her approach for the night. Without jamming herself into any more revolving doors, she was confident she could bring Jackson Kent to heel.

The room phone rang and it was the front desk, checking in to make sure that everything was to her satisfaction.

"Yes, I'm pleased. Please thank your manager for the gesture of the upgrade. It was—"

Lilly smiled as the clerk explained that the room was not only complimentary for her stay but that Mr. Jackson Kent himself had asked that they guarantee her satisfaction.

"Oh. How very generous of him!" Lilly indulged in a little shimmy of victory. *Humiliation—who knew it would be such a lovely opening move?* "I'll be sure to ring if I need anything."

She hung up and surveyed her room with a new appreciation. Lilly was confident that the race was half way run. Any man who'd pushed them to upgrade a room was sure to expect the key; and she was just the girl to slip one in his pocket and invite him up for a bubble bath. She'd interrogate him naked if she had to…

But in the meantime, the space was still hers. The luxury suite lacked for nothing and she intended to enjoy every amenity she could while she was "off the leash". Corporate control was nothing to sneeze at; and she loved the illusion of freedom that field missions gave her.

A demon could forget almost anything when they were out in the human world.

Except that they were a demon.

And that freedom was strictly forbidden.

Chapter Three

Girl-Next-Door was not her strongest gambit but Lilly was confident that even her "B Game" rivaled Marilyn Monroe on her best day. In the privacy of the elevator, she gave her shoulders a little shimmy to summon her energy and renew her focus. The beaded dress was heavy artillery but the body inside the dress was a weapon of mass destruction.

"Brace yourself, big boy. Here comes the pain." The elevator doors opened and Lilly sailed out, a temptress on the move. She smiled at the inevitable stares from every man in her peripheral, savoring the power of causing no less than two of them to walk into walls.

She barely looked at the brass easel holding a large poster board outside the double doors, making a passing note that Jackson's name was on it. *I'm in the right place. Okay, intimate cocktail party is about to get—*

Lilly stopped in her tracks. The intimate cocktail party was a massive event that filled a ballroom that was barely shy of being the size of a town square. Three hundred people milled about around table tops decorated with acrylic "ice sculptures" that glowed alternately in whites and blues. A giant banner that read "Ice and Snow Charity Gala" was strung across a stage that was also decorated in glittering white silks and sumptuous silver chiffons.

"What the—"

"Hey, pretty lady!" A man approached her with two cocktails containing ice cubes that glowed in alternating pulses of blue and white. "I'm gonna buy you a drink and see if I can't get you to buy me!"

Lilly's brow furrowed. "Pardon me?"

"The bachelor auction!" He held out one of the hi-balls. "What do you say? I'm quite a catch, baby."

"I say only an idiot walks around looking like a blue light special and announces that he's a bargain. It's an open bar, so that would make that drink free. And I—I am many things, sir, but free is not in the description." She stepped around him without looking back. *Disaster. The agenda in my mission file said 'small cocktail party to kick off weekend'. This. This is a mob scene and I am not wearing the right clothes!*

People were dressed up for a fancy night and cocktails but she was a shimmering black beacon in a sea of white and blue eveningwear. Her fingers curled into fists at her side. *Damn it! There was a white and blue theme to the attending guests?! Black puts me in the scorched column because someone is getting a memo to melt their eyes out of their skulls for this screwup!*

Lilly did her best to gather her wits and see if she could still recover anything from the evening. She scanned the room for Mr. Kent but stayed on the move. In a crowd like this, standing still was an open invitation for any man brave enough (or who'd had more than two drinks for courage) to make a run at her. Women at the party were also taking note of her, some with admiration but others with open hostility as she presented the worst kind of competition—Lilly looked like a woman who didn't follow the rules and human females had an instinctive aversion to the trait.

Relax, ladies. Claws in. I'm just here for a quick mission and I have no interest in your men. Trust me, you can keep them.

Lilly crisscrossed the space without success and began to accept that retreat may be her only option. Her instincts were infallible and her quarry was not in the room. Apparently his name on the banner was the only bit of him present, which meant he was probably more of a figurehead than an actual participant in the charity. She mentally noted it as a potential clue as to why the poor man had been flagged in the first place for—

"You look lost."

She turned at his voice and hiccupped in surprise. *Impossible!* "I'm—okay. Maybe." She stopped herself and then nearly howled in frustration as a very undemonic squeak escaped her lips with yet another hiccup. "I am not lost. I am here—*squeak!*— for the charity event this weekend and just between us, I'd like to meet you without feeling—*squeak!*—like a clod."

"You feel like a—clod?" Jackson asked.

Lilly put a hand on her hip, defiant. "I never get the hiccups."

"Never?"

Squeak. She pressed her fingertips against her lips, caught in a strange trap of fury and frustration. There he was. The man she was about to seduce and destroy with her delectable feminine powers and she had….*the hiccups*?

Since when? If someone in the Corporation is playing a practical joke, I'd say I am not in the mood for a laugh.

In desperation, she stole a glass of ice water from the nearest partygoer without a word and downed it before the man could protest. She set the glass down, took a deep breath to ensure that the worst was over and squared her shoulders to face Jackson again. "Never."

He laughed. "God, you're fabulous!"

Lilly struggled with her composure. "Fabulous?" It was a first but she forged ahead to make the best of yet another rough start. "I have a different definition of that word."

"Okay. Let me just say that I'm the one who qualifies as a clod. I meant to get your name this afternoon and—"

"Mr. Kent," a woman in a modest dark blue ballgown came up behind him. A wireless headset and tablet in her hands immediately conveyed her role. "We're cued up and ready to go."

"Just give me a few minutes, Laurel," Jackson started to put her off.

"I'm sorry. No. The webcast is set and we'll be transmitting an empty stage to the online community of supporters if you don't get in position." She cast a knowing and dismissive look in Lillith's direction. "There's just no wiggle room on the schedule, Mr. Kent."

"Damn it," Jackson swore under his breath but Lilly took it as a good sign. If he was frustrated to leave her side, it meant she was making headway after all. "I am so sorry. Please. Don't go anywhere, okay? I'm going to get this right, I'm going to get your name and we'll—"

"There's really no time," his assistant cut him off, stepping back to lead him toward the stage. The girl called back over her shoulder, "I'm sure if the lady is a registered attendee and wishes to spend time with you, she can always bid in the auction!"

Lilly smiled. What a lovely suggestion! Since it was clear that pretty little thing would sabotage any casual meeting on his radar...

"Good evening, everyone!" Jackson Kent's voice came over the stereo systems and she immediately spotted him up on the stage behind an acrylic podium. "Welcome to the Ice and Snow Gala to kick off our Snow Angels Foundation's fundraising weekend!"

The room burst into applause and the guests settled in for the entertainment ahead.

Jackson went on. "I want to thank you all for your generous support of Snow Angels and I won't go into the pitch right away. As you know, there'll be plenty of time for you to hear about the work we are doing to add that critical care wing onto the children's hospital and to build a family support center. Oh, trust me," he joked, "you're getting the pitch! But for now, let's enjoy the evening and see if we can't let the ladies kick things off this important weekend by demonstrating what true generosity looks like and how beautiful giving can be! And of course, a big thank you to all the bachelor friends of mine who," Jackson cleared his throat before continuing, earning laughs from the room, "*volunteered* themselves for the cause! I've been informed you can't have the cold without the heat, so let the Bachelor Auction begin!"

Applause circled the room and an aura of anticipation began to build as large screens in the room displayed a few glamour and beefcake shots of some of his friends who would be up on the block.

When Jackson's picture popped up, there was a surge of applause and a few squeals of excitement in the crowd, but for Lilly, her entire game plan fell into place.

"Onto the rules! Ladies, you will bid on your bachelor and then he is "yours" for the weekend! Now, what that means, is up to the pair of you to negotiate, but let's just say that for the rest of the event, I will be very disappointed to hear that any winning bidder had to carry her own drinks, open a single door or worry about finding a dance partner!"

There was more good-natured laughter, but Lilly stayed focused. The rules were ridiculous but she was taking it all very seriously.

"And I don't want anyone to feel left out! Gentlemen can bid too if you're a fan of a certain sports announcer or hockey player or you have always wanted to have the ear of a famous movie producer, my friends are happy to hang out and share stories or even hear a pitch or two." Jackson winked at the bachelors in the wings and one of the Hollywood actors standing closest. "Just please don't ask Roger to take his shirt off. He's shy, people."

"Oh, and the wrinkle!" Jackson continued. "We are opening it up to our online attendees so if they outbid the ladies in the room, then it's very possible, that so long as no laws are broken, our bachelors will be agreeing to head out for a private dinner date with their winning bidder at a later time and place."

A new ripple of excitement moved through the crowd. It was all for a good cause but the notion that the long table of cell phone wielding auction employees could steal a prize out from under their noses added to the thrill.

Lilly kept her expression neutral but she was a demon in her element and if any creatures were known for their competitive streak and a love for games, it was the employees of Hades Enterprises, LLc. She retrieved her phone from her small metal evening purse and made a quick inquiry to the office.

Budget? She texted before glancing up to make sure that she had time before Jackson was up.

The first bachelor stepped out onto the stage, some All-American slice of he-man that had several women jumping to their feet to start screeching out numbers. Lilly simply watched, allowing the rhythm of the bidding to flow and absorbing the playful trappings of the auction. There was a great deal of laughter as some bachelors fared better than others and when one very sweet man whose bio proclaimed him to be a professional hockey player and a chef was won by a very generous woman dripping in diamonds who appeared to be two hundred years old; even Lilly began to smile.

Her phone vibrated a response and she quickly activated the screen to read the reply.

UNLIMITED.

Lilly stared at the word. It was not what she'd expected to see. She'd been looking for a number, not some bizarre and uncharacteristic proclamation of a blank check. Not that money was generally ever an issue for Hades Enterprises, LLc. It was the running joke of the Corporation that the only reason H.E.LLc did its own banking (and Heaven, Inc.'s while it was at it) was that it didn't trust anyone on earth even with the ridiculous amount found in their petty cash drawers. Money was nothing more than a mortal construct but the Corporation tried to respect it and not jeopardize things by getting too playful with the game.

UNLIMITED.

Lilly kept looking at it. *Unlimited? Okay, Mr. Kent. Whatever you're into, they want you badly in Upper Management because this is a first.*

Lilly shut off the device and tucked it securely away. An agent did not question the mission but it was hard not to wonder what offense the poor man was guilty of to earn the bulldozer full of hurt coming his way.

She folded her arms and patiently waited as the contestants dwindled until it was finally the auctioneer bachelor's turn up on the block. Jackson Kent reluctantly stepped up onto the makeshift dais.

"Okay, let's face it. If I don't go for more than a fast food meal, I'm going to be crushed," he joked, immediately rewarded by laughter. It was obvious that things were orchestrated for their host and founder of the charity event to go last for good reason. What fascinated Lilly was that he didn't look very pleased up on stage, as if he would prefer to keep out of it.

Too late now, Mr. Kent.

"Can I start the bidding at a thousand dollars?" he asked cautiously.

"Five thousand dollars!" A woman's voice rang out, and the tension in the room was broken by applause.

Lilly's attention diverted to the challenger. She was attractive enough in her white mini-dress to pose a minor threat and Lilly decided that the time for quiet had passed.

"Wow! Thank you!" Jackson said. "Do I have another bid?"

"Six thousand," Lilly called out.

Jackson put up a hand to try to shield his eyes from the lights to see his bidders, but gave up when things suddenly took off.

"Ten thousand!" the same woman countered and several by-standers cheered her on.

Lilly was alone but she didn't need a cheering section to win. She just needed to top any number her rival spit out. "Twenty thousand!"

There! That should shut her up and—

"Twenty-five thousand!"

Damn it!

The woman began to jump up and down, anticipating her own victory.

"Wait! We have a call in bid for seventy-five thousand dollars!" One of the men shouted in from the phone table.

Gasps echoed around the room and then more applause, as the mini-skirt sat down in a harumph of defeat. Several guests glanced over at Lilly and even mouthed their condolences as the evening's drama began to draw to a close.

"Oh, wow! Seventy-five thousand dollars? That's incredible!" Jackson conceded with a smile. "Okay. I'd say it's time to say, going once, going twice, and—"

Lilly narrowed her gaze and decided she didn't have the patience for another round. "One million."

There was no applause.

Silence rippled out as everyone in the room held their breath.

"Would you mind repeating that bid?" Jackson asked into the microphone, openly stunned.

"One million dollars." Lillith didn't have to raise her voice for it to carry, then smiled as she realized that he really couldn't see her because of the stage lights in his eyes.

"Going once, twice and sold!" he said quickly, setting off the crowd's approval and a roar of laughter and applause at the insane amount she'd uttered. "Now just because we've hit quite the number there, folks, does not mean any of you are off the hook for the rest of the weekend," he said. "I mean it! I'm going to pitch you harder than ever because now I really have hope that we can get the new family support center open and change lives! And we can do it in record time if you'll step up, friends!"

He waved to them all. "Okay, enough of that! Drink, be merry and enjoy the rest of the evening while we get this dance floor opened up!"

Jackson Kent exited the stage, his assistant meeting him at the foot of the stairs.

"The webcast is bound to go viral with that last bid and we'll use the publicity to increase the windfall. You handled it well—"

"Well? I nearly started to cry!" Jackson amended, waiting for his eyes to adjust to the dimmer light. "My God, that was surreal! Who was that? Was that Margaret Bonner-Blair? I knew she had deep pockets and had threatened to show but..." Jackson ran a hand through his hair. "I need to give that woman a hug!"

"Just a hug?" His mystery woman stepped forward in the wickedest black beaded dress and Jackson froze. "Seems a meager reward considering..."

He'd been so distracted with the hiccups and the water and—God, how did she keep surprising him? And how had he not noticed that dress a few minutes ago? "You haven't met Margaret Bonner-Blair." He was teasing but he needed to catch his breath. It wouldn't do for the winning lady to catch him with his tongue on the ground, but there was something about this woman that completely fried his inner circuits. "Quite the wild show, I guess. What an amazing finish!"

"I'll admit I never saw it coming."

Miss Marsh stepped up, tablet in hand. "I hate to keep doing this to you, miss, but Mr. Jackson needs to locate his winning bidder. We're going to need a photo of the pair of them to post immediately." Laurel sighed. "Hope she's up for all the attention the press is going to give her."

"Oh. No photos."

"Pardon?" Laurel asked crisply.

Jackson felt as if someone had just poured warm caramel down his spine. "You? Don't tell me that was you!"

She stopped moving toward him, her expression one of total confusion, her cheeks turning a disarming pink. "Okay. It wasn't me?"

"Mr. Kent, I believe the bidder was closer to the center of the room. Let me just ask my spotter in the sound booth." Miss Laurel Marsh was nothing if not efficient in her quest to locate the winner.

Jackson dug in his heels. "Wait. Let me try this again. I'm sorry. I'm just—I'm not that lucky. Was that—did you just bid a *million* dollars for me?"

Mystery goddess nodded, a smile lighting up her face. "I did. It was a bit of an impulse purchase."

"An impulse purchase?" Jackson felt like jumping up and down but he forced himself to try to play it cool as if it were every day that the most beautiful woman in the world dropped lottery money into his charity's buckets—and as if his heart weren't already threatening to beat out of his chest at the sight of her in that black beaded dress.

"If you're about to tell me that there's a disclaimer and anyone who can't get through a revolving door unbruised isn't qualified to bid, I guess I can help your assistant track down Ms. Bonner-Blair and see if she's up for it." She playfully crossed her arms but the gesture only accented her rocking cleavage and made everything on his body start to sing.

I can't believe this is happening. I'm turning into a high school freshman yammering at the prom queen!

"Oh, you are qualified to bid!" Jackson held out his hand. "Just tell me your name, please."

Miss Marsh lifted her tablet and gave Lillith a look of open challenge, as if to say, *If you don't think I'm googling your ass the instant you open your mouth, lady, you have lost your mind.*

Lilly smiled. Rabid administrative assistants were hardly obstacles and she knew that Benjamin's IT trench work was as masterful as any on Earth. "The last name is Fields."

Laurel Marsh's reaction time was impressive. "I don't show a Fields on the guest list of registered attendees."

What the Hell?! I'm going to kill Benjamin for missing such a simple step!

"Really?" Lilly's surprise wasn't disingenuous.

"Then the list is off. Miss Fields, it's a pleasure to meet you and…" Jackson cleared his throat. "Um, it is miss, isn't it? Or was that an openly telling prayer that you aren't a Mrs. Fields?"

She laughed. "What kind of married woman would be tossing out a fortune to spend the weekend with another man?"

Laurel's gaze narrowed dangerously. "You'd be surprised."

Lillith deliberately ignored her and kept her eyes on Jackson's. "I am unmarried."

"And how would you like to make that donation?" Laurel asked. "We have forms to fill out and naturally there's the necessary process of—"

"Laurel!" Jackson pivoted to face her, his displeasure impossible to hide. "Is that how we thank someone for their generosity? Because if we're growling at all our donors about forms before we've even said a kind word, I think we need to ratchet that down immediately."

"The transfer's been made, Miss Marsh," Lilly intervened smoothly, delighting in the change of color in the woman's face. "Check the accounts and you'll see it. I took the liberty of using my phone's bank app to make the payment the instant I won. No time like the present, right?"

"Apps are all well and good and I'm sure when the banks re-open on Monday it's more likely to—" Laurel's jaw dropped open on cue as her tablet chimed her with an online message regarding a certain seven-figure addition to the charity's account. "That's impossible! But—I'm…Thank you so much for your prompt and—it was just such an astonishing amount I…"

Lilly shifted her attention back to Jackson. "Are you worth a million dollars, Mr. Kent?"

He humbly shook his head, raising his hands in surrender. "Is any guy?"

Lilly blinked. He'd just passed up the perfect opportunity to puff up, swagger around and say something slimy about how he'd be worth every penny or offer to show her his best.

She shook her head slowly. "I'm not the woman to ask."

"Can I get you a drink, Miss Fields?"

"Only if you're planning on joining me and having one as well." Lilly deliberately shifted her weight on her feet, a subtle move that made every shimmering bead on her dress come alive to accent her body. "I can drink alone for free at this shindig, Mr. Kent."

His breath caught in his throat and she knew the visual effect wasn't lost on the man. "There is no chance of that happening, Miss Fields. I meant, having a drink alone, here or anywhere I suspect."

She smiled to soften the edge and was instantly rewarded. "Could we have that drink away from this crowd? Would that be too much to ask for my million dollars?"

"That sounds like a very reasonable request to me. I may be many things, but I'm no fool to miss a chance. I can't go too far before they send out search parties but the bar in the lobby looked fairly empty earlier." He took her arm to escort her toward the hotel's bar, away from the crowded gathering. "Okay, I may have overstated it. My mom always said the first hint that a man's an idiot is when he announces that he isn't an idiot, Miss Fields."

"It is counter-intuitive, isn't it?" she joked as they walked together. Lillith quickly incanted a demonic deflection prayer in her mind to give them an added measure of privacy. The other guests in the hotel would see them but wouldn't recognize the celebrity in their midst as quickly—it wasn't perfect but it might give her a few more minutes alone with him before a fan dared to approach for his autograph. Then again, Lilly didn't think she'd need more than a few minutes of good conversation before they were racing upstairs. She repeated the incantation in her head one last time and smiled. It was old magic but Lilly like most employees in the Gambit was reluctant to trust technology alone.

And certainly not luck.

"That looks friendly enough for a quiet drink over there." Jackson smiled. "Please tell me your first name otherwise I swear, I feel like I'm a boy in school if I have to keep calling you Miss Fields."

"Lilly."

"Lilly." He amended himself then smiled. "Your name is Lilly Fields?"

She shifted out of his hold and crossed her arms defiantly. "Lillith. But yes. Would it make you feel better if I pretended that you were the first to make that clever connection?"

He sobered instantly. "I'm sorry. That was—not my best moment." The humor of the moment undermined him and he smiled. "I love that you have that name. It suits you somehow."

"More than Roxanne Fierri or Serena Craft?"

"What?"

"Sorry. It's just when I fantasize that I have a different name, I like to aim for something more sophisticated than a lame version of Poppy Meadows." Lilly dropped her arms. "I'm convinced that a woman named Roxanne would not get trapped in revolving doors so my next move will be a legal name change. You're the first to know."

"Thanks for keeping me in the loop." He retrieved her hand and led her to a comfortable pair of leather chairs by the bar's fireplace. Jackson signaled the waitress to order a bottle of red wine and two glasses as they settled in. "I guess I better get to know you before you disappear into witness protection."

He waited until she was seated before taking the chair across from her and Lillith marveled at the show of chivalry. Then again, most men she met would already be asking her to sit on their laps, so any change was a pleasant surprise. "I'm a tough woman to track, Mr. Kent."

"Whoa! First names. I thought we'd made it to first names, right, Lilly?"

"Agreed." She deliberately gave him a shy look. It was all progress and it was all familiar ground. Lillith reveled in the sensation that the reins had finally landed firmly in her hands. "Jackson."

Time to play a game I know.

The wine came and two generous glasses of ruby liquid materialized in their hands. Lilly took a sip from hers, savoring the flavor and potent effect of the alcohol. Demons didn't get drunk. They couldn't if they tried but a light buzz was always pleasant and could provide an illusion of vulnerability. "Does anyone call you Jack?"

He shook his head. "No. I hate nicknames and I don't know how I got around it, but here I am. Just Jackson."

"Truthfully? No Jacko? Jackie? Jack? JK? Jay K? Jay?"

He theatrically winced with each variation. "You're making me want to cry," he joked then sampled his own wine. "Okay, names established. What about you, Lilly? I want to know everything about you."

She blinked. "I haven't even finished my drink yet."

He laughed. "Sorry. It's just—ever since I saw you in that giant blender of a door, I want to take a crash course in everything Lillith Fields."

"A crash course?" Lilly arched her back to accent the lines of her figure enjoying the chase again. "As Dean of Admissions to the Fields School, I am pleased to inform you that I am currently taking applications. Naturally, we'll need an interview and possibly an essay or two before you get a pass, sir."

"Damn, why do I suddenly feel unprepared?"

Because you are. "Jackson, I met you five hours ago and we've had less than ten minutes together, but you don't strike me as a man who is unprepared. Ever."

"I *was* in the Boy Scouts," he conceded.

"Were you?" She gaze narrowed as she leaned forward. "Was it a formative positive experience or one that you've had to pay for therapy to overcome?"

He laughed again. "It was great. I am an Eagle Scout and have a box of badges to bore you with. How about you? I'm strangely not getting a Campfire Girl vibe from over there, Lilly."

"No?" Lilly set her glass down. "Okay. You got me. Not a badge to show but I do know how to tie knots like a sailor and I think I can start a fire in a survival situation and keep you warm in a blizzard."

"You mean, if my life depended on it…you could make a fire with two sticks?"

"Absolutely." Lilly's show of confidence faltered as his eyes met hers. "Well, I might need a few more items."

"Like a flint or steel wool?"

"Like a lighter."

She won another laugh which triggered a delicious cascade of tickling warmth inside of her. It was a ridiculous sensation but Lilly tipped her head to one side to study the man who evoked yet another surprising thrill for her. It was selfish and foolish but she decided that she would steal as many of these moments as she could for her own pleasure.

And to win. I will naturally just make him smile and laugh to win.

"So are you telling me you're a pyromaniac?"

Lilly shook her head and tried to refocus. "Jackson, I know the clock's ticking and now it's been nearly fifteen minutes of intense bonding but I don't think I can bare my soul to someone I know nothing about. I'm a little nervous about kicking off the sharing."

"Really? You don't look nervous, Lilly."

"I am and I have every reason to be. You want to know everything about me? So I—what comes next? I start spilling about food allergies or my life's most embarrassing moments?"

"Isn't that usually how people get to know each other?"

"Normal people. But you're a celebrity and I'm…" She picked her glass back up. "Mystery is the only edge I have right now so if you don't mind I'm going to cling to my fleeting advantage for just a few more minutes."

"Okay, Lilly. Mystery looks really good on you, by the way."

"Which doesn't give you a pass, Kent. Your turn then to start spilling."

He shook his head. "That's not fair. Besides, my life's an open book that apparently everyone has either already read or already guessed at."

"I haven't read it and I am a terrible guesser."

Some of the warmth fled from his eyes. "This is really starting to feel like an interview."

"My bad. There's always the essay option but if you just hand me a copy of a magazine article about how you like to work out, I'll be very disappointed, Jackson."

"I hate to disappoint anyone."

"I wonder…" Lilly sighed. "I wonder if you aren't rusty at this portion of the playbook, Jackson. You're so used to being introduced in the first paragraph of a magazine article, you may have forgotten how to do it yourself. And if you expect every woman you meet to have already read your biography and memorized your statistics, it's a bit of a loss, isn't it?"

"You haven't read my bio?" he teased but she could see a flash of pain in his eyes. She'd hit a tender spot.

"Nope." She smiled and took another sip of her wine. "I warned you I'm a terrible guesser, but let me give it a shot if you are too shy."

"This should be good."

"You are Jackson Kent. You are very fit and enjoy drinking those squishy electric green shakes that people make by putting vegetables and fish paste into blenders for breakfast and have a secret addiction to kelp pancakes."

He laughed. "I hate nutrition shakes and have an aversion to any combination of the words 'fish' and 'paste'. Tell me that's not a real thing, is it?"

"It's a delicacy in Japan."

"I love Japan but remind me to really ask what I'm eating next time I go."

It was her turn to laugh. "Check. Doesn't like fish paste. Okay, back to guessing." She squared her shoulders. "In the off season, you play in a garage band and plan on putting an album out this summer after making your public debut at the Austin Music Festival."

"I'm tone deaf and am pretty sure that there is a restraining order out there to keep me at least fifty feet away from karaoke machines or any public attempts at singing." Jackson shook his head. "People would pay for me not to sing, Lilly."

Lilly rewarded him with a playful pout. "I told you I was a terrible guesser. I had one more about you going out for the Olympic curling team but I hardly see the point."

He nodded slowly. "Curling does look like a longshot but I'd take it over golf as a sport any day."

"Tell me one true thing about yourself that I won't find in that open book," she said softly.

"Like what?" he asked cautiously.

"Tell me your favorite color."

His eyes widened and his smile was a bone-melting sight as his shoulders relaxed and the defensive fight left his expression. "Blue."

"What kind of blue?"

"Like the ocean."

"That's eight thousand different shades of blue."

"Exactly."

Lilly refilled his wine glass. "I'll allow that answer to stand on a technicality."

"I'll take the pass." Jackson shifted in his chair. "And openly rejoice at how easy that was."

"Why?"

"Pardon me?"

"Oh, please. You gave me hiccups. I never get the hiccups, Jackson. *Never*. So let's pretend you don't have the upper hand and that it will take more than a fluffy claim to liking the ocean to win."

"You're not the only one experiencing a few hiccups, Lilly. I'm not sure when it's ever good to tell a woman that she makes you feel like a freshman crushing on Miss Universe and that the only reason he isn't glibly telling you all about himself is pure terror."

"Terror?"

"Terror because I think you, Miss Fields, are an all-or-nothing proposition. Publicists make everything shiny. What if you aren't really interested in the boring reality behind those stories? I guess one thing is true. I'm a competitive soul and I hate to lose and looking at you, I have the weirdest sensation that the stakes are impossibly high."

Lilly smiled. "Risk terrifies you?"

He shook his head very slowly, never taking his eyes from hers. "Only before I jump."

She radiated an unspoken invitation without moving so much as an eyelash. "One…two…three…"

He sat up straight and reached for her hand, an impulsive gesture that won him more than he bargained for because Lillith was a goddess to look at but touching her was—Jackson's breath stopped in his throat. His fingertips slid over the bare skin of the back of her hand and it should have been nothing. It should have been a single moment that a guy experienced and later couldn't recall in a day of much more striking moments. But actually touching Lilly for the first time was apparently a thing he was convinced he would remember until the day he died.

"Lilly."

Oh, hell. Don't kiss her. Not cool or smooth or wise or…what kind of jerk pounces on a woman in their very first conversation? When have I ever been that kind of guy? When…shit….brain off….

For the first time in his life, he did exactly what he knew he shouldn't, ignored the clamor of an alarm in his head and simply jumped. He stood and pulled her up into his arms, tipping her head back and claiming a kiss. If he'd hoped for one taste of her lips, he hit the jackpot with a thousand sensations of raw primal heat. Kissing this woman wasn't an appetizer. It was a feast that silenced every alarm or logical voice he had in his head. She responded without hesitation, without surrender and without mercy.

It was only when he heard someone behind the bar drop a glass that he remembered where he was. Jackson lifted his head, gasping for air, and more than a little mortified at the loss of control. *Can't...take that back. Hell, I don't want to!*

"Oh, my!" she sighed, her eyelashes fluttering as her eyes opened to look up at him. "That was...worth every penny."

Shit.

Jackson released her instantly. "Shit."

"What? What did you say?"

"No! I didn't say—I shouldn't have done that." Jackson stepped back slowly and she did the same, the atmosphere between them suddenly tense and awkward. "I'm so sorry. I mean I'm not sorry that happened but I think I'm sorry for..."

"For the record," Lilly said as she crossed her arms again. "That is *not* the reaction any woman longs for after a man kisses her."

"No!" Jackson stepped back up, drawing her against his chest. "For the record, that was the most amazing kiss I've ever shared with a woman and I was six seconds away from admitting that and then throwing you over my shoulder to haul you upstairs to my room and..."

"Six whole seconds? You were going to wait six whole seconds?" Without really moving, he felt as if she were melting into him, as if every nerve ending in his body was attuned to the one and only goal of bedding this woman.

"That. That was not the take away from that speech." Jackson took a deep breath. "Public bar. Mauling you in a public bar is not the way I'd like to initiate anything this amazing and... Damn it. Lilly, I can't take you upstairs."

"Can't?" She froze, the intensity of her gaze unwavering. "Why can't you? Is it a medical condition? An STD? Is there already a harem upstairs in chains you don't want me to see?"

He smiled at the quirky twists of her sense of humor. "Lilly! You just donated a million dollars to my charity in a bachelor auction. Tell me you can see how that makes what's happening between us more than a little complicated?"

"More complicated how?"

Jackson ran his hand back through his hair. "This charity is near and dear to my heart and your generosity...is overwhelming. I could never thank you enough for your contribution. But if the tabloids got wind of this, I don't know how to spin it so it doesn't look like you paid to play."

"The money is going to the charity, right? Not some offshore account you have in the Caymans, so who cares how it looks?" Lilly reached out to place the palm of her hand against his heartbeat. "Maybe no one is looking."

An avalanche of regret undermined his joy at her touch. "If there is one thing I've learned over the last few years with online gossip columns, twenty-four hour sports channels and the vortex of every human being you see having a video camera in their pockets and the ability to post anything and everything they want to the internet...I've probably blown it already. Lilly, someone is *always* looking."

"I'm not going to argue against that one." Lilly sighed.

"Let's...just...let me see if I can find a path through this mess, okay? I'm not a genius but I do know how to throw a Hail-Mary."

"I don't know what that is, Jackson. Does it mean you'll think of a way to kiss me again?"

"Kissing you again is only the first item on the agenda, Lilly."

"Okay, then. Hail away and I'll see you tomorrow morning." She smiled up at him and then lifted up onto her tippy toes to kiss him on the cheek. "Thanks for the wine. You go and I'll cling to my dignity, sit here and pretend I commanded you to go."

Jackson inhaled her perfume as he bent over to help her with the gesture and wished he were more of a villain because the path upstairs was sinfully wide open. She was soft heat and firm curves and every seductive thing that made his body tighten up with desire, but there was something more to the mysterious Lilly than a gorgeous exterior.

At the moment, it was all he could do to breathe through his frustration. Of all the women to make an amazing contribution to his charity! The press would have a heyday if he were caught creeping out of her hotel room after that bid. Money had changed hands. There was no way he didn't end up looking like the world's most expensive male escort. But God help him, he was determined to find out about Lillith Fields and to discover a way to make her his own without some tabloid twisting it into garbage and chasing her away.

"I could limp to make a more pitiful show of it."

"That would be much appreciated." She smiled at him and he leaned over to return the gesture and kiss her cheek, but even that contact unraveled a firestorm inside him and guaranteed an embarrassing retreat as his pants remained painfully tight against a stiff and raging hard-on.

"Good night, Lilly." Jackson had to invoke the self-discipline of a lifetime to walk away, but he couldn't stop grinning like a fool. Because no matter what temporary obstacles existed, nothing really mattered. He'd just met the One and what idiot complained about a damn thing when life hands you the greatest prize in existence. This weekend, he would be a gentleman and prove to her that he wasn't playing.

He'd take his time, and then by the time the press was involved, it wouldn't matter. Then if they wanted to paint him like a fool in love, he'd be happy to let them.

Oh, yes.

Jackson Kent was all in.

Lilly sat down slowly and watched him walk away. While normally she'd enjoy the view of his delicious backside in eveningwear, the circumstances were robbing her of her objectivity. Because what the man wasn't doing was hauling her off to his room.

This was a new wrinkle.

She'd put her best shot across his bow and practically glowed with the 'come and get me, big boy' vibe. Even more encouraging, he'd gone for the bait and come in for a kiss. Now, in her experience, that was the point of no return for a man. One kiss was all it took for them to throw common sense over their shoulders like spilled salt and turn into mindless apes. One kiss and she was the one holding the reins.

Except for Jackson Kent.

One kiss and she was the one mindlessly ready to climb him like a tree, a giddy version of a temptress she had never been before he'd touched her.

Lilly's brow furrowed as she weighed the implications of it all and tried to sort it out. *He's simply prettier than any target I can remember, that's all. I am after all, a creature of lust so why wouldn't I eventually find a sexy man a pleasurable temptation all his own? It means nothing. I should take it as a good sign that I can still feel.*

She sighed, calmed at the explanation and set aside the mystery of her own desires and then refocused on the next issue at hand. Jackson Kent who clearly wanted to bed her was going upstairs without her.

Winning him in that auction had had repercussions Lilly hadn't foreseen. Now it looked like paid sex and that was a hard line for the boy to cross. Mr. Kent was wary of the appearance of impropriety and he didn't want any misunderstandings in the press or between them.

Damn it. I think I just paid a million dollars to be the one woman at this shindig he can't shag. Talk about expensive chastity belts...

Lilly stared into the fire blazing in the nearby hearth to center her thoughts.

Improvisation was her forte so the answer came quickly. "There is nothing more compelling than a woman just out of reach. So for a twist, we'll just let him wrestle with a problem of his own making." And in the meantime, Lilly would make every effort to be as tempting as possible and always nearby so that when he weakened, she could pretend to run.

If Jackson Kent was hoping she would support his moral choice by acting more circumspectly and wearing turtleneck sweaters, he was in for a rough ride.

Lilly leaned back in her chair to finish her wine just in time to see Miss Laurel Marsh take a few tentative steps into the bar. Laurel was scanning the crowd apparently looking for her missing employer.

Lilly raised her hand to get the woman's attention and was not oblivious to the flash of relief in Laurel's eyes when she saw that Lilly was alone and that Jackson had eluded his bidder's nets.

"Miss Marsh! What a delight to see you again!" Lilly gestured her over to the fireplace and Laurel complied with crisp civility.

"Yes, and you, too." Laurel held out a thick packet with the Snow Angels Foundation emblem embossed into the folder. "I thought you might want one of these. Every registered attendee should have received one when they checked into the hotel but it didn't look like you'd picked yours up. Your name badge is inside."

"Oh, I don't wear name badges." Lilly took the awkward gift with a smile. "But thank you. I think my check-in was a little unconventional this afternoon. It's perfectly understandable how the staff might have forgotten it after I broke their front door."

"You...broke—?"

Lillith waved the question off and abruptly opted for a subject change. "I don't want to relive it. But I'm touched that you would go to this trouble, Miss Marsh, with everything on your plate to leave the party and track me down just to bring me the charity's packet."

"Oh, well, I was also looking for Mr. Kent. The party is winding down but I thought he might want to make another appearance." Laurel pulled out her tablet and held it firmly to her chest like a shield. "Do you know where he is?"

"He just left and went upstairs to get off his feet. So, you're officially off the clock! Would you like to come and sit down with me and have a drink?"

Laurel hesitated. "I should call his room and make sure he's set for—"

Lilly's look of horror shut her up. "You. You need a drink, woman. By all means, pop back into the ballroom to make sure the deejay you hired hasn't resorted to playing the electric slide or the chicken dance but I don't think Jackson would be pleased at a phone call. He'll take back every nice thing he said about you, Laurel!"

Laurel's defenses bristled but then fell. "He said nice things about me?"

Lilly smiled, signaled the waiter to bring them another bottle and subtly accepted victory as Laurel took the vacant chair by the fire. "He thinks you're a walking miracle of organization. But he'll take it back if you yank him out of a hot shower or wake him up to tell him when you're going to wake him up. Come on. Relax for a few minutes. No one's looking."

Laurel's expression was one of wary gratitude. "I have been running full steam since about four this morning."

"Wow." Lilly's eyes widened. "You are either the most dedicated person I have met—or the craziest."

"I take my assignments very seriously." Laurel straightened her shoulders, a touch of pride in her stance.

The bottle was delivered to the table and the wine was poured. Lilly smiled. Laurel had the drive of a demon and while it was the ultimate compliment, she doubted Miss Marsh would be happy to hear it.

"Are you freelance or do you work solely for Jackson? Because if you're freelance, I shall have to get your card before the weekend is over." Lilly lifted her glass for a sip of her wine. "So long as you don't expect me to be up and running at four."

"I freelance and if you want to, you can sleep as long as you'd like. I'm a personal assistant, not a drill sergeant." Laurel held out a business card, a crisp offering that demonstrated that she didn't need a weekend to pass before she seized the opportunity to make contact with a potential employer. "Here you are."

"Another career choice you may want to consider though," Lilly teased as she dutifully took the card. "Just warn the military before you make the change."

"Everyone needs a back-up plan." Laurel smiled and took a measured sip from her glass.

"I hope Jackson doesn't wear you out doing too many of these events. Is it a marathon or a sprint?" Lilly asked.

"For me, it's a sprint. This is my first event with him though his full time assistant hinted that his job resembles non-stop marathons." Laurel sighed and set her glass down. "His assistant came down with the flu at the last moment so I stepped in."

"Oh! She must be so disappointed to have missed this!"

Laurel shook her head. "*He* was very disappointed and more than a little shocked. Apparently Mark is never sick and his husband told me that keeping him in bed has been nothing short of world war three."

"I imagine if a person is used to juggling twelve things at one time then sitting still and doing nothing must be akin to torture." Lilly lifted her glass. "Keep up, Miss Marsh. It's rude to make me drink alone."

Laurel dutifully retrieved her glass and took a healthy swallow.

Aha! Don't like to back down from a challenge, do you?

"I have to say your boss isn't at all what I expected." Lilly tipped her head to one side as if making a study of her competition. "Is he what you expected?"

"I never create expectations of people to avoid disappointment. But nothing about Jackson Kent is a disappointment. Not that I would say anything negative about a client even if they were a nightmare walking!" Laurel took another sip from her glass to recover her composure. "What were you expecting him to be like?"

Lilly shrugged her shoulders. "It's hard to say. I always expect people to be disappointing. I'm used to nightmares walking. Trust me. What I've seen puts nightmares into a completely new category."

"No offense, Miss Fields, but you don't look like a woman that anyone would ever give a hard time much less nightmares. Every guy in this bar looks ready to pledge their lives to get your next drink…"

Lilly didn't look around to confirm or deny the attention she was receiving. Instead, she kept her gaze steadily on Laurel. "Maybe but since I can buy my own drinks, what do I care what a man thinks?"

"Wow. Go, girl power." Laurel leaned back a little, admiring the flex of strength and character. If Lilly read her correctly, Laurel Marsh valued her independence and talents above all. But she wasn't immune to loneliness and she was clearly smitten with Lilly's target.

Laurel hasn't slept with him yet. But she wants to…

"Laurel," Lilly began again. "Is Jackson Kent religious?"

Laurel shook her head. "I don't think so. If he is, he's not showy about his convictions. I've never heard him say anything overt and he's never flashed it after putting points on the scoreboard like some guys do. That's not to say he isn't privately an intensely spiritual person."

"Hmm." Lillith took that in, wondering again what Kent had secretly done to get Upper Management's attention. Private spirituality didn't usually draw fire. Usually it was a hypocritical demonstration so blatantly offensive that even the Corporation was forced to raise its eyebrows. High profile Take-Downs were not as common as most people hoped. Lilly sighed. *Of course, thanks to modern tech and celebrity egos, most of the bigger targets take themselves down before we can get there.*

The rules of a Take Down were fairly simple. There was no framing a target, no planted or manufactured evidence and no photo-shopping allowed. The human being had to actively expose their own weaknesses, make a choice that led to their destruction or voluntarily confess the worst in a public way that ensured that whatever power they'd falsely achieved was forever gone. A Temptations Agent could be the catalyst, advisor, mentor and in some cases, the siren drawing them toward the rocks but they couldn't turn the wheel. In other words, a demon on a sanctioned mission could point your vintage thunderbird toward the ravine, but they couldn't drive the car off the cliff's edge.

If the lines became murky, if there was any confusion about directives, Lilly would contact her supervisors and await instructions, but she hadn't done that in over a hundred years. She took pride in her independence and ability to improvise. She was in no mood to forfeit the bragging rights of a successful career that spanned millennia.

"Are you a huge sports fan, Miss Fields?"

Lilly took a sip from her drink. "Why do you ask?"

Laurel's eyes were not warm despite the charming expression she mastered. "Oh, I was just curious. So many women have become interested in the game in the last few years but their interest is limited to the men's measurements, the pictorial spreads in magazines and the ever popular underwear ads. It's so demeaning, don't you think?"

Lillith's demonstration of shock was perfection. "Jackson Kent has been in an *underwear* ad? Voluntarily or was he blackmailed into it? Did he lose a bet?"

Laurel's mouth fell open. "What? H-He...No, he did not lose a bet! I'm sure he was—very well paid and…" Miss Marsh recovered as best as she could. "You're having me on, Miss Fields! Every woman on the planet from eighteen to eighty bought that magazine when it came out with Jackson's ad!"

"Did *you*?" Lilly asked innocently.

"Of course not!"

Lilly just looked at her and waited.

"Well, I saw it naturally! It was on every billboard and building for weeks last summer. You had to be blind to miss it!" Laurel began to rearrange her drink and purse, a woman clearly about to make a run for it.

"Oh, don't go. I was just teasing." Lilly reached out to touch the woman's wrist, a subtle gesture but it was skin on skin. Women weren't her specialty but she knew the general principles of touch. *Calm, Laurel. I just want to talk.* "I spent a million dollars to get what you already have, Miss Marsh."

"What I have? And what do I have that's worth a million dollars?"

"Jackson Kent's attention." Lilly let go of Laurel's wrist and smiled, then shrugged her shoulders as if in defeat. "Oh, well. It was worth it just to see the expression on his face at the donation. I am a satisfied customer."

"I'm—as I said I am his personal assistant for the event. That's all. And trust me, you have his complete attention for the remainder of the weekend, Miss Fields. In fact, I'm a little surprised you are here in this bar alone considering…"

"No one owns me!" Lilly refilled both of their wine glasses. "We are modern women, Miss Marsh!"

"Yes." Laurel missed the transition and then gasped as all her progress to finish her wine evaporated in front of her as the challenge was reissued. "Who knew?"

"You strike me as someone very comfortable in command." Lilly shook her head with a laugh and raised her glass to encourage her new friend to partake. "I'm not keeping any man on a leash no matter what the price tag. Besides slavery is against the laws last time I looked. The auction is just a fun game for charity. Mr. Kent will take my coat or make sure the waiters aren't forgetting to bring me drinks but I didn't buy the man!"

Laurel mirrored the toast and took a small sip. "No. You did not."

"I'm far more interested to hear about this hospital and the plans for that family center. How did Jackson get involved? Does he have financial ties to the company that owns it? Is he dating a woman on the hospital's board?"

"I don't know. I am not—even if I were privy to that information, I would not be at liberty to say." Laurel's brow furrowed, her ethics pushing back at the interrogation. "Are you a reporter?"

"With a million dollars to spend on four minutes of a man's time?" Lilly's eyes widened. "My God, how much do they pay those people these days?"

Laurel winced. "Sorry. I was…that was a stupid thing to ask."

"Not stupid."

"It's just that there is almost nothing about you on the internet, Miss Fields. I'd expect a woman who can spend a million dollars like that would have her own page in Wikipedia." Laurel's cheeks were pink but she wasn't backing down. "Seventh graders in Iowa have bigger online profiles, Miss Fields."

"I value my privacy and I spend a lot of my resources to keep myself to myself." Lilly beamed. "It's my one and only eccentricity. Besides, what good does Google do me when I'm this backward? I'm practically standing in a hole next to you! I spend a fortune for a handshake and a brief conversation but I miss a chance to spend less than ten bucks and see him in his underwear? Who does that?"

At last, she won Laurel's laughter and the tension between them was gone. Lilly sat back and began a careful campaign of alcohol and feminine camaraderie that would uncover every scrap of information Miss Marsh might have on a certain sexy athlete and get Lillith what she desired most.

It's first and goal, Miss Marsh, and the clock is running.
Hike!

Chapter Four

Lilly was up before dawn the next morning. For all her protests to Laurel about an aversion to mornings, she rarely wasted any time when on a mission. Sleep generally constituted lost hours and fatigue was rare. Demons had mythic stamina but an envious fascination with human beings' talent for dreaming. Demons did not possess the power to dream which made real sleep an elusive concept for most of the employees of Hades. They rested and recharged but they did not truly sleep.

So of course ironically they loved elaborate rituals that surrounded the chase for dreams and any demon worth their salt could tell you the exact thread count of any bedding from fifty paces.

She watched the wintry landscape slowly come to life through the giant window that framed the luxurious view and placed a call into Benjamin smiling at the ridiculous speed of his pick-up.

"Lilly! Is he down?"

"Good morning, Ben," she said. "I'm fine. Thank you so much for asking. No, the weather isn't nearly as Siberian as we were dreading and yes, I will be sure to steal you a hotel robe."

"Sorry," he countered, except he didn't sound very contrite. "Look, I'll update the weather report and be sure to check Aspen off on my 'places demons hate to visit' database but for now, humor me. What's your status? Is the target almost down?"

"I am in position and I have his attention. Last night was just a warm-up and an opening mixer. Today's Friday and the first official full day of the weekend event. Can't a girl take her time and enjoy one for once?" Lillith began to go back through her wardrobe choices for the day as she spoke. "There's an evening dress I'm dying to try out but if I show up in the damn thing for a breakfast buffet, I think I'll be overdressed so I'm definitely stretching it out until after tonight."

"Something's up, Lill."

"Why? Did someone tweet about my bid and cause a stir?"

"A few ripples about a million dollar mystery woman but for the most part, we've been ordered to dampen the blaze. The video of your big winning auction moment got suppressed before the human techs could do anything with it so the story has no meat yet. The angle if someone asks is that you prefer to remain anonymous and they have no permission to release photo or video but if your guy double checks their footage you are blacked out. I think our Management might be saving up the raw video as ammo if it plays better after you find out what he's hiding. But I can't make sense of any of it. It's tense over here."

"Maybe but tense or not they covered that million dollar transfer without a blink, Ben. They can't be that antsy."

"Asmodeus has been called upstairs twice and there's a rumor on our floor that Malcolm is requiring regular updates on your mission. Something's up."

"Malcolm? The Regent is personally tracking *this* mission?" Lilly blinked. *Why? Why would the Regent of Hell be interested in a routine Take Down? What in the world is going on?* "Ben, keep your head down but I need you to find out why."

"I'll do what I can." The sound of Ben's keyboard coming to life made her smile. He was talking and typing, and it was the most comforting thing in the world to her. Ben was as reliable as a sunrise and he wouldn't let her fail.

"I think we're both overreacting, Ben. Perhaps the Regent is just impressed with…our department's efficiency, or our teamwork." Lilly smiled at her own pep talk. "Let's not forget how awesome I am."

Ben didn't laugh. "Get it done, Lilly. I've checked the signal on your phone and I'm keeping you on a constant lock if this thing goes south."

"It isn't going south. Stop saying that. Why do you suddenly sound like a very bad version of a Kremlin spy in an old film?"

"Sorry. Of course. You've got this. Just take him down and then press the black button on your phone for immediate retrieval. I upgraded the app to make sure it's a clean extraction."

She rolled her eyes, grateful that it wasn't a video conference. "You are starting to sound like an old woman, Ben. A really weird old woman."

"I don't care. I'm worried and I don't like anything about this mission. Where's the hook?"

"I have this. He's nothing special. I didn't realize taking an extra day or two to play was going to cause such a ruckus."

"You're sure there's nothing about him that's…off?"

"Relax. It's probably something he's hiding in plain sight. Do me a favor and drill down on the hospital board and corporations behind them. Any chance there's an attractive woman in that sphere that we might have missed? See if there's a connection that could have been overlooked in a quick pass and then go back again over Kent's personals. If there is someone special on the board itself or some scandal behind the scenes then I'll have what I need. Does he have an illegitimate kid out there in the big wide world with cancer? There has to be something, Ben, but I can't waste hours in front of a computer screen at this point. Do a full sweep of his business interests and financials for me while you're at it, okay? I need to get ready for a breakfast and see if I can't charm the man over coffee and scones."

"I'm on it. The original files are nearly blank and they don't appear to have gone too much further afield than his credit reports and bank accounts so the hospital thing may do it. Maybe he's embezzling funds? Not exactly your usual kink but ugly, right?"

Lilly closed her eyes, frustration tightening around her skull in a vise of pain. "At this point, I'll settle for ugly."

"Why is the top floor watching this, Lilly?"

"I don't know but I need you to start smiling. Nod your head and act as if I've just told you the best damn insider tip you've ever heard. If you look worried, you're only going to feed that rumor mill, Ben. Do me a favor and on your next break make a point of saying that maybe I'm taking a weekend of spa treatments just to steal a paid vacation."

"Demons don't get paid vacations."

Lilly rolled her eyes. "I know, Ben. It was a joke. Remember humor? Damn it, I need you to get on board the giggle wagon, partner, and help me out."

"Okay. You got it. I'm a grinning fool."

"Great." Lilly sighed. "Just what the doctor ordered."

"Be careful."

"I'm a Temptress. It is Jackson Kent who needs to be careful." She hung up on Ben without another word, struggling with a storm of fury and fear at the betrayal of her department's confidence in her skills.

I don't know why but if the top floor is watching then I am going to step up my game and take him down completely. There'll be nothing left. Damn it. Whatever you're hiding in that black hole of a heart, Jackson Kent, show it to me!

**

Jackson finished his workout, grateful for the physical release but also the side effect of a renewed sense of calm and purpose. A long hot shower only cemented his great mood.

Focus, Kent.

Except he didn't feel distracted. Kissing Lilly had galvanized him in ways he wasn't sure how to voice.

He was going to hit every mark he needed to for his event and the charity he'd spent years building to support Snows Metro Hospital. He had a meeting with the coordinating team before the breakfast downstairs and then a full day of scheduled appearances and activities. The fund raising was off to a flying start but instead of slowing down or resting on his heels, Jackson was more determined to use that momentum to make this weekend even more successful for the pediatric ward. Hell, if they pushed every attendee to step up and catch benevolent fire with the energy and possibilities of participating in a charity event to end all others—the hospital's support center and new wing could be state of the art and provide services far beyond one city.

Lillith Fields.

God, she had inspired him in so many ways. She was all woman, all siren, and all he had dreamed of... Her act of generosity had challenged him because he wondered if he hadn't been thinking too small with his goals. And on a very personal level, he wanted to prove to her that he wasn't just an empty celebrity shell. He'd keep her close and let her see him in action doing what he loved and hopefully in the meantime, he'd win more than one weekend with her.

Hell, if he could he was going to see if he could convince her that he was after more than a one night stand. She was so warm and responsive, it was hard to hit the brakes.

He'd just finished pulling his pants on when the hotel phone rang.

"Hello, this is Kent."

"Good morning, Mr. Kent. I know it's early but we didn't have a chance to review the agenda for today and—"

"Laurel," he cut her off as gently as he could. "I'm up. I'm ready whenever you are. Just let me—"

A knock at the door made turnabout fair play.

He opened the door still holding the phone only to be faced with Laurel Marsh on the other side.

"No time like the present."

"O-okay." He stepped back to let her in and then followed her into his suite. "I'm not sure why I thought I was going to have time to put a shirt on, but let me see if I can't rectify that first. Sorry."

Laurel's blush at the realization that her boss was half naked would have been endearing if not for the tight press of her lips into a thin miserable line. His assistant was not happy. "Certainly. Shirt first."

Jackson grabbed one of his favorites, suitable for the morning ahead and also put on his best game face. He admired Laurel's efficiency but he missed Mark's sense of humor and timing. "Okay, I'm buttoned up. Would you like a cup of coffee? They sent up a big pot this morning and I didn't touch it."

Laurel sat at the table by the window and began to pour herself a cup. "Nectar of the gods!"

"Late night last night?"

Laurel froze, a potential source of her unhappiness revealed. "I *never* drink when I'm on the clock and *rarely* when I'm off it but I had the bright idea of spending a little time with our largest donor to see if I could…" Laurel sighed miserably. "I don't know how much wine I had because the damn glass never really got empty. But apparently I did a lot of sipping!"

"You spent some time with Lilly?" he asked. "To what purpose?"

"Mr. Kent, you hired me to help you make this event a success. I came in at the last minute, so I don't know what screening process or vetting you did on your VIP guests and that woman is… I can't put my finger on it but Miss Fields is not what she appears to be."

Jackson swallowed a surge of defensive anger and did his best to keep his tone level. "She appears to be a very generous person and a friend to this charity. What are you seeing?"

"Nothing."

Jackson's anger wavered as confusion entered the fray. "So this pout about Lilly is based on nothing?"

"I mean I am seeing *nothing*. She is not on any list of expected attendees that Mark gave me and there is no record of a Lillith Fields getting an invitation to this very exclusive weekend. It's previous donors, board members and hospital trustees and supporters and VIP friends and friends of friends but this wasn't exactly a "tickets available online" affair. I don't have an address, an email address, contact information, zippo for Miss Fields."

"A friend could have slipped her their invitation and she's made the most of the opportunity." Jackson crossed his arms. "It's not exactly illegal to crash a party and not after you've more than paid for your ticket."

"So who is she? I asked her directly about the goose egg I got when I did a casual online search. She brushed off the invisible woman trick she has going but the Queen of England doesn't have the resources to pull that feat off! There is *nothing* on her anywhere. It's as if she dropped out of the clouds, Mr. Jackson. I think it's a con of some kind."

"A con?" Jackson blinked hard, trying to take it in. "Laurel, did her donation hit the charity's accounts or not?"

"It hit. Instantly, which is insane if you think about that for more than a minute. An electronic transfer would be flagged as pending for at least twelve hours until they could verify the accounts during business hours. I shifted her donation over to another account to make sure it was legitimate and the darn thing rolled without a hitch. Snow Angels Foundation is officially one million dollars closer to that family facility." Laurel sampled her coffee and then went on. "The money is real even if she isn't."

"She's real. So she prefers to remain anonymous and gave us a different name. That's not a crime."

"Not a crime but not exactly above board either! What does she have to hide? I don't see any other millionaire or billionaire at this party sashaying around giving fake identities out. Even the audio and video from the party last night of her winning bid mysteriously got erased. I checked with the team this morning and there was some kind of technical issue with the equipment—but only when Miss Fields was on screen. This is like KGB level weird or that secret vampire fighter club in that bestseller."

"Wacky conspiracy theories aside, I'm going to just blame a lack of coffee for that last suggestion." Jackson shook his head. "Look, technical problems happen and I can't remember the last time half my friends checked into a hotel with their real names. Unless you love the paparazzi or random fans visiting your room at two in the morning, you get smart fast. It's all a coincidence at this point."

"My spidey senses are tingling," Laurel muttered.

Jackson smiled. "Cons are about getting something, Miss Marsh. Not giving money away. If she's a con, she's the worst one in the history of history."

Laurel's pout was not pretty to behold but it was heartfelt. "She's—hiding something! And she has a lot to gain and you seem to be too humble to see the obvious payoff here. I think she's angling to cash in on her investment and win Jackson Kent for keeps. From where I'm sitting that woman looks like a professional trophy hunter and you…"

"Yes? Me?" he prompted her to finish what she'd started.

"You look like a deer in the headlights."

He crossed his arms and waited. His temper flared but he wasn't going to jump. Laurel might mean well but Jackson was not happy to have someone insinuate he had the street sense of a toddler. From the inner city of his childhood neighborhood to the temptations of college for a rising sports star and the landmines for a professional, he had navigated them all and was *not* wet behind the ears—especially when it came to women.

And Lilly was not a trophy hunter.

Not that he knew much about her for certain. He was navigating blindly on instinct and when it came to Lillith, probably on hormones. But he didn't care. He wasn't going to get puppy slapped by his personal assistant for who he chose to see.

"Sorry," Laurel conceded miserably. "I overstepped."

Jackson took the seat across from her and finally remembered to finish buttoning his shirt. "Thanks. I'll ignore the inference that I'm some helpless kid who can't see a train coming. But Lilly isn't a train and I don't care if her real name is Hilda Boobenschmitz. I like her. A lot. And since I'm so far past the legal age where a man gets to make his own calls, let's just say: I'm touched by your concern, I won't be looking to you for approval and I don't need my personal assistant's sign off on anything I do."

"Yes, sir."

"What I do need is your discretion and your help. Lilly's winning bid is a great excuse to spend what time I can with her and I'm looking forward to every minute of it. But I also want to stay on schedule and make sure everyone is having the best weekend of their lives. I can't neglect my duties as host and the tournament on Saturday is going to be a bear to run even with the great team we've got managing all our volunteers."

Laurel nodded, sobering as they shifted gears in the conversation. "I've moved Miss Fields to your table for every meal and party. Mr. and Mrs. Watts made a point of asking for a few quiet minutes with you. I added it to your online schedule for after breakfast. I understand they also have a gorgeous check they want to give you away from the crowd."

"See? Not everyone wants to make a public show of it."

Laurel's grunt was something in between a scoffing snort and a laugh. "Sure. Do an online search on Mr. Warren Watts and see if those hits are higher or lower than a hundred thousand and then we'll talk, okay? Moving on, Mr. Kent."

"Moving on."

"If you'll hand me your phone, I'll add the new alerts. Which means if your phone starts chiming, you need to be ready to move, Mr. Kent."

"I'll do my best. But I've never been a fan of pagers, Laurel."

"Don't kill the messenger." She began to add the alarms and events to his electronic calendar. "And I know the subject is closed but feel free to text me a 911 if the feminine crazy train leaves the station and you realize you're riding first class."

Jackson rolled his eyes but started to laugh. "Sure. You're the first person I'll contact. I mean what guy doesn't live for the epic 'I told you so' that move is going to win me?"

"Better embarrassed than murdered by some rabbit boiling psycho heiress," Laurel muttered.

"I heard that, Marsh!"

"Sorry." She handed him back his phone with an expression of sincere contrition and began her retreat. "I'll see you in the coordinator's meeting downstairs in fifteen minutes."

"With bells on." He walked her to the door. "You be nice to our donors, Marsh. That means *all* of them."

"Yes, sir. You'll have no complaints." Laurel was through the door and it closed firmly behind her before he could think of a way to soften the awkward snap in her eyes.

Jackson leaned against the door and sighed. Three days. All he had to do was get through three days without losing his footing and then anything and everything was possible.

Three days.
How hard could it be?

Chapter Five

To contrast with the previous night's onyx beaded bombshell, Lilly deliberately chose the opposing color palette. The woman in the mirror was a creature sheathed in creamy white palazzo pants and a cashmere wrap sweater edged in fur she was a luxurious modern snow queen. Not that she intended to actually touch snow.

She eyed the agenda from the packet that Laurel had given her and reconfirmed that snow was something she could avoid without too much effort. Tomorrow was the big outdoor ski tournament where she planned on playing the part of the sexy spectator. But today looked lighter with free time in between each meal before a formal gala in the evening. Lunch was the presentation about the charity and would be the only overt sales pitch but she would make sure she was there to keep Jackson off balance and happy.

"To Hell with the office," she said on a slow exhale. It was time to show them all how the game was played. If she came in too hot, he might just run for the nearest exit. So today, she would be the delectable and well-behaved philanthropist of his dreams. At least, until she convinced him that some lines were drawn just for the pleasure of crossing.

She left her room and made her way to the large banquet hall where the breakfast buffet had been laid out. She accepted a mimosa from one of the waiters and began the search for Jackson in a casual pattern that covered the space. Several men nodded to catch her eye or smiled but she politely kept moving.

Always a good choice. Although, a little tougher to maneuver since there are way too many people staring! Damn it, there'd better not have been another color theme to the dress code because I will have Benjamin's head on a platter to—

Laurel Marsh approached with her signature crisp efficiency and interrupted Lilly's internal tirade. "Miss Fields. How is it that I am running on half-speed and barely upright today after all that wine and you...? You look unfazed and way too gorgeous for this hour."

Lilly smiled. "And how is it that you always make a compliment sound like an accusation? It's a dangerous gift, Miss Marsh, but to answer your question, I try to stay hydrated."

"Sorry. Jealousy rears its ugly head."

Lilly laughed and then looked back across the room to catch no less than four women in the act of snarling about her or staring daggers. "You're forgiven. Just tell me if the seating is assigned or should I just make a run for the table closest to that chocolate fountain?"

Laurel shook her head. "It is assigned seating and I can take you up to the head table if you'd like." Laurel began to lead her through the tables. "I'm afraid we lost the video of your bid last night. So much for viral gold," she sighed. "But perhaps we could take a few pictures this morning to—"

"No photos," Lilly cut her off. "Oh, look! There's an omelet station. I'm famished!"

"Yes," Laurel said brightly to hide her disappointment. "No need to stand in line, Miss Fields. The wait staff will bring you whatever you want and…here we are. Head table!"

Lilly realized that a name card awaited her at the head table next to Jackson. The sight pleased her. She'd hoped he'd make good on his word to keep her close and well attended, million dollars aside. Appearances demanded civility but after that kiss, he should be a man abandoning civilization very, very soon. "This is perfect."

A waiter took her order and she sat back to relax and survey the room for—

"Ah! Miss Fields," Jackson greeted her as he came up to the table just behind them and Laurel left without another word to give them a moment alone. "I was hoping you wouldn't mind joining me for breakfast this morning."

Lilly's smiles sizzled with heat to mask her surprise at not seeing him coming. "I would never mind sharing breakfast with you but in my fantasies, it wasn't this crowded."

Jackson laughed. "I had the same wicked thought. But let's make the most of it, shall we?" He pulled out her chair and helped her get settled before taking his own place. "I'm doing my best to behave, Lilly."

"Did you have a good night's sleep, Mr. Kent?"

He grinned at her like a boy at the opening of a game. "I slept like a rock!"

She blinked, her own cheerful demeanor cracking a little. "Like a rock? Are you serious?"

"Dead serious. After an hour long ice shower and a dose of allergy medicine that would have taken down a small village, it was as if I'd been carried off by cherubs into the land of Nod."

Lilly laughed. "Now that's more like it! A man kisses me and skips off? I need to see dark circles under those eyes at the very least. I want sweet retribution, sir."

"I've never been happier to admit to misery then." He shook his head with a gleam of humor in his eyes. "Anything to please a lady."

Lilly leaned in confidentially. "Anything? Are you sure?"

It was a thrill to watch his internal systems lock up as his brain's primal drive dictated that he was *very sure* and *very ready* to please her in any and every way he could think of. The color in his face changed as he struggled to remember where he was and why he couldn't allow impulse and instinct take over.

"Jackson!" Another guest interrupted the volcanic moment as they took their seat. "Best spread ever and may I compliment you on a great event, dude!" He winked at Lillith and she assessed a handsome and overly-confident mortal man openly making a play for Jackson's table mate. "I'm so impressed that I'm going to be writing checks left and right and I haven't even gotten the full court press yet!"

Lilly smiled innocently at the newcomer. "Maybe that's his strategy. He keeps us all relaxed and guessing until the last moment."

"I had to come and meet the Million Dollar Lady." The man extended his hand to take hers.

"Offering to match her donation?" Jackson asked. "I understand women are impressed by that sort of thing, Stefan."

The actor blatantly ignored him and continued to press forward for his introduction to Lilly. "I'm Stefan Walker, but you probably recognize me."

Lilly shook his hand. "I'm Lillith Fields. Have we met before?"

The man's mouth fell open a little. "I'm…Stefan Walker."

"Yes, you said that already." Lilly let go of his fingers even as she summoned a bit of demonic charm to make sure that the ridiculously famous film star was enthralled. "Are you on the board with Jackson at the hospital? Or just a supporter of the foundation?"

Jackson's laughter and look of possessive pride confirmed her strategy. "Ha! Stefan! Apparently not every woman breathing has a thing for British vampire spies."

Lilly pressed her fingertips against her lips, pretending embarrassment. "I'm so sorry. Are you a British vampire spy, Mr. Walker? That's an awkward thing to put on a business card."

"Really?" Stefan preened then shot Jackson a challenging look before he settled into his best Hollywood persona for Lilly's attention. "I never thought I needed to bother with cards."

Lilly laughed. "What good villain ever does?"

"You think vampires are real?" he said, his voice almost a purr as he mistook his own sexual interest for hers.

"No. They are the stuff of fairy tales but if you are delusional, I don't want to be the person to spoil it for you." She leaned in slightly and lowered her voice. "Or to be the one to tell you that you aren't really British."

The man's jaw dropped as he'd been doing his best imitation of a posh Oxford native. "Wow!" He abandoned the ploy for his native drawl. "Most women never blink and just love to play along—at least until the next morning, right?"

Lilly blinked as if he'd burped. "Do they? Well, how comforting to know I'm not the only one making an effort not to hurt your feelings."

"Ouch." Stefan straightened in his chair. "The lady has claws."

Jackson cleared his throat. "If she's showing them, it's because you're being a jerk. This isn't one of your fan fests and I think you're trying a little too hard, friend."

Stefan did his best to take the setback in stride. "No worries. I like her all the more for it. It's refreshing to meet a woman who isn't shoving her panties into my pockets. Come on, though." He shifted his focus back to Lilly. "Are you saying you really don't know who I am?"

Lilly tipped her head to one side and studied him. "Would it make you feel better if I did?"

"Would it make you retract your claws, kitten?"

Lilly's smile brightened. "Sorry to disappoint you. I'm afraid Mr. Kent is probably right."

"Right about what?" Stefan asked.

"You're trying too hard." Lilly smiled. "I'm happy to meet one of Jackson's friends though—even if he is a British vampire spy on television."

"I'm in films and you'd have to live under a rock not to know that," he said, cutting her off. "The size of that donation you made, I thought you'd appreciate the celebrity treatment."

Jackson started laughing and couldn't stop. The sight of the most egotistical lady-killer on the planet wilting like a wallflower under Lilly's innocent barrage was priceless. Walker was an acquaintance via one of his biggest contributors and had only come because there were a few Hollywood movers and shakers at the event he'd wanted to schmooze, but Jackson wasn't a personal fan. Even so, to watch Lilly shut the guy down—it was like watching a touchdown. He hadn't thought it was possible to like her more, but she kept surprising him and resetting the bar.

Oh, man. I'm going to propose before Sunday if she keeps this up.

Lilly sobered but Jackson could see the sparkle of wit in her eyes. "That was the *celebrity* treatment? Is the pouting when I didn't recognize you the highlight or are you working yourself up to tears? I admit, I do love to see men cry."

"Keep the claws, little lady. It's clear you need them," Stefan countered snidely and then straightened to look out over the room. "If you'll excuse me, I think I see someone worth saying hello to over there."

He strode off without another word and before Lilly could make a joke about the importance of being earnest, Jackson was starting to get out of his chair with a growl. Lilly caught his forearm and stopped him. "Jackson?"

"That was uncalled for. He'll apologize to you, Lilly." Jackson's expression was grim. "But first I'm going to have a private talk with Mr. Hollywood."

"Jackson Kent." She tightened her grip on his arm. "May I say one thing before you head over there and make a scene?"

"Maybe?"

"I'm flattered at your defense of my honor but if tabloid fodder and a disaster is going to happen, please can it happen because you carry me out of this room over your shoulder to spend the rest of the day naked in your hotel suite? I mean, beating up one of your guests is another way to go, but I fail to see how my suggestion of sensual delight gets shot down but Mr. Walker gets to wreck things and I still get jilted… Any ideas here?"

Jackson smiled, the tension leaving his body as he settled back into his chair. "Well, that put it in perspective."

"If you want to get him back, just walk up and make a show of putting a pair of your boxers in his pocket at the ball tonight. Tell him it was the British accent that did it for you," she suggested wickedly.

"You, Miss Fields, are quite the trouble maker."

"You have no idea." Lilly sighed happily. "But confess, Kent. Do you have a temper? Are you prone to fights in public? Have you ever killed someone in a bar fight? I need to know for my own safety and well-being."

And because a violent jealous temperament could prove useful.

"No to all of the above," he said. "Never really felt the urge to punch anyone like that before… I think you bring out the cave man in me, woman."

The grip on his arm transformed into a subtle caress. "I'll let you get a good grip on my hair and haul me around…and we can learn to communicate with grunts and primal noises." Lilly shifted her hips to pivot toward him keeping her seat but effectively shutting out the rest of the world. "What do you say? My cave or yours?"

"You're killing me, woman." He covered her hand with his, the intensity of his gaze sending shivering spirals of heat down her spine. He leaned over to make sure no one else could hear him. "I was supposed to stand up and say something in the way of a welcome to the crowd—and now there is no way I can stand up without showing off just how much of a cave man I am."

Lilly rewarded him with a sympathetic sigh and then shook her head. "I'm steering you off course, aren't I? Sorry. For the record though my goal for the day was to play hard to get and show off just how cool I can be. This was supposed to be my zero flirtation demonstration to impress you with my self-discipline."

"Wow. *That* was zero flirtation?"

"You're killing me, man." She echoed his words playfully and then primly turned back toward her plate as one of the waiters delivered breakfast fit for a queen. Other guests joined them at the table and the moment was lost as Jackson was forced to make small talk with his largest donors and pretend they weren't both in a sexual bind.

Lilly pushed her food around and tried a simple breathing exercise as her consternation grew. Because instead of dismissing the heat between them, she was having trouble reining herself in. Her innate gifts worked against her and her awareness of his heartbeat and body's warmth was making it hard to think straight. She could hear his breathing and knew from centuries of practice just how far she'd pushed him.

What rattled her is how far she'd pushed herself and how her own body was refusing obedience. A Temptress was not supposed to get tangled in her own net but with Jackson the lines were blurring and she didn't like it.

She entered into harmless small talk with the other guests at the table, deflecting their questions with a pretended interest in them or by asking about their connections to the charity. Lilly applied herself to charming them all and ignoring the pull of the man at her side.

"—slopes, Miss Fields?"

Lilly blinked and realized she'd just missed what the woman next to her had said. "Pardon me?"

"I asked if you were planning on hitting the slopes, Miss Fields?" the woman repeated sweetly, a vague Southern accent adding to her charm. "The snow is the perfect powder today."

"Oh, no!" Lillith took a sip of her mimosa and read the woman's name on her table tent. "I never ski, Mrs. Rickett."

"What was that?" Jackson's attention shifted to her so quickly she immediately realized her mistake. "You don't ski? How is that possible? I mean—the revolving door when you got here. Your skis got caught in the door."

Lilly laughed and set her drink down. "I was going to try it. Bunny slopes and humiliation to round out an adventurous weekend but after my glorious entrance, it doesn't take a soothsayer to read the signs! I'm the last woman who needs to slide down a mountain on her rear end before she accepts her limits."

"Oh, dear!" Mrs. Rickett interjected. "Well, there is plenty of après-ski fun to be had, isn't that true, Mr. Kent?"

Lilly batted her eyelashes at Jackson. "I *am* looking forward to fun away from the slopes, Mr. Kent."

Jackson had to clear his throat before he answered. "We do aim to please."

"I'm going to count the hours until the Fire Ball tonight," Lilly sighed. "Are you going to ask me to dance, Mr. Kent?"

"Oh, but you'll see him before then," Mrs. Rickett offered, apparently oblivious to the undercurrent of desire between her host and her seatmate. "You can't miss the lunch today! We'll get to see the plans for the center and I do look forward every year to Jackson's presentations."

"Not as glamorous as the ball tonight, but I do hope to see you there, too, Miss Fields. The lunch talk is kind of the heart of the weekend," Jackson said softly. "And I wouldn't miss that dance with you later for anything."

"Not even for a million dollars?" Lilly teased and then regretted it.

Jackson's smile faltered and Mrs. Rickett audibly gasped. "I nearly forgot about that incredible bid of yours! That was such a wonderful thing you did!" she said.

"It's just money," Lilly said. "I…If I were smarter, I'd have done it anonymously via that bank of phone lines they'd set up against the wall."

Jackson's eyes met hers and she sighed with relief.

"Hindsight is usually humbling," Jackson offered. "But I wouldn't change a thing."

Lilly pushed the eggs around her plate, unsure of what to say. Flirty banter was limited by their seatmates' presence and she wasn't sure progress was possible as Mrs. Rickett's interest was firmly set on her.

"I'm gonna make sure Mr. Rickett knows that since he can't win prettiest donor, he better gird his loins and get his checkbook ready if he still wants them to put his name on a bronze plaque at Snows Metro anytime soon."

"It isn't a competition," Jackson said. "You tell George we're happy with any check he cares to write this year and if he wants his name on a bronze plaque, I'll talk to the hospital board. You both have been so kind since the beginning, I'm embarrassed I didn't think of the plaque myself."

"Aren't you a dear man!" Mrs. Rickett laughed. "But don't you dare cave in that quickly! You make that man keep writing checks for at least another ten years because I for one, love seeing him really try for once in his life." She shifted to pat Lilly's arm. "Some men truly need a challenge to be happy, don't you agree?"

Lilly nodded knowingly. "Though some men are the challenge, aren't they?"

"Not for you, I should think."

Lilly knew she'd meant it kindly but her demonic sense of humor was faltering. She wanted to say something saucy about no man truly presenting any challenge with a trained temptress in play but her failure to bring Jackson Kent to heel was a little too raw. "Oh, I've had my share of setbacks."

"I can't picture the man who wouldn't melt into a puddle at the first bend of your little finger."

Funny, you're sitting across from him…

"Me, neither," Jackson added, "but let's let not embarrass Miss Fields any further. Or me if I have to admit I'm melting like a snowman in July over here."

Laurel's return to the table to stand at Jackson's elbow was simultaneously a relief to Lilly and an irritation. The personal assistant was nothing if not efficient when it came to interruptions.

"I'm so sorry to push in but Mr. Kent, the manager wanted to talk to you about some of the arrangements for tomorrow." She held out her tablet as if to back up her claims with the notes she'd made. "He's worried we've overbooked the lifts and he wanted to see if you'd like the third slope reserved."

Jackson pushed back from the table reluctantly but Lilly recognized the set of his shoulders. He did not take his responsibilities lightly and he wouldn't complain about his commitments no matter what he would prefer to be doing at that moment.

"Excuse me, everyone. I'll be right back to—"

Laurel shot him a look that made him amend his promise.

Jackson smiled and shook his head. "Looks like I'll see you all *at lunch* for the presentation. I hope you enjoy your mornings," Jackson gave Lilly a look that conveyed his regret. He leaned in close to whisper in her ear, "I'm going to see you on those slopes, Miss Fields, if only for the chance to catch you when you fall."

"Good luck with that," she replied softly. "I don't do snow, Mr. Kent."

"We'll see."

He straightened up with a wink and then headed out with Laurel trailing after him. Lilly sighed.

I should have talked her into tequila shots instead of wine last night and given myself a little more freedom to maneuver.

She waited only as long as civility demanded and when she couldn't push her breakfast around the plate anymore without feeling ill, Lilly excused herself to make a quick exit from the room. She made no eye contact with any of the other guests, disinterested in small talk or the potential tangle of any of the men mistaking her natural saunter for an invitation to play.

A temptress was already a natural troublemaker but one currently experiencing her first remembered bout of sexual frustration—Lillith knew she was practically glowing with a 'come hither' vibe that was hard to rein in. And just in case she hadn't known it, there were no doubts before she made it to the doors as conversations halted and more than one husband got a firm pinch to regain his attention and turn him back in his seat.

She walked quickly along the edges of the lobby and then took the stairwell to avoid the elevators. She checked her phone as she climbed, scanning Ben's report again just in case she'd missed anything. But if anything, the man was looking more and more saint-like with every re-read.

"Okay, Kent. Maybe it's not here. But you know what they say in Hell's kitchens. Stick to the recipe in the cookbook and if you can't find the ingredients, wait for them to find you." She refused to allow the office's panic to disturb her plans and rush her into a bad move. The luncheon did not sound like an opportunity to do more than push chicken salad around a plate and endure power point presentations but Lillith didn't have the luxury of throwing away any opportunities.

A touch of demonic magic made the flights of stairs feel like level ground and she was fresh and unfazed by the climb when Lilly reached the upper floor to her rooms. What she didn't expect was to see Stefan Walker standing outside her hotel room door, knocking on it and then trying to peer through the security peephole below the brass numbers.

Chapter Six

She stood behind him, quietly taking in the sight of Hollywood royalty with his face pressed against the wood in the worst impression of a ninja she had ever seen.

"Am I just hiding in there after realizing it's you lurking outside my door? How rude of me!" she offered to enjoy the comic sight of him leaping back, a child caught in the act.

"I…was…I came up to apologize." He shoved his hands in his pockets and attempted his most heartwarming look of heroic contrition. "I think my ego got in the way of meeting an incredible woman and I couldn't let that happen."

Lilly assessed the hallway's emptiness and forced a smile to her lips. She was truly beginning to dislike Mr. Walker. "Oh, no. It didn't stop you from meeting me. And don't trouble yourself. It also didn't prevent you from having my panties tucked into your pockets." She leaned over to drop her voice to a whisper, "There was *never* any chance of that happening."

The endearing expression on his face evaporated. "No one believes that, Miss Fields. You have the look of a woman who can't spell the word 'no' much less use it when a real man steps in your path. I don't know Kent very well, but he's way too much of a choir boy for what you need."

Lilly sighed and subtly pressed a button on her phone. "Didn't you get the script, Stefan? You ask. I say, no thank you. Then you become more charming and win me tomorrow at the ski tournament by humiliating yourself with the children, demonstrating your hidden humanity with your kindness and evoking my tender side when you seal it by writing a check for a million dollars before whisking me away to your private island. See how easy that would have been?" She recrossed her arms defensively. "You trying to improvise, Ace?"

"Unlock your door, invite me in for a drink and you'll see."

Lilly shook her head firmly. "No. No kidding. That's a solid no." *I'm not interested in watching you drink anything that isn't spiked with bleach at this moment, guy.*

Stefan lifted one arm to lean against the door frame, as if he were posing for a camera shoot. "Look. I thought it over and I figured you out. You paid a million dollars for Mr. Clean and from the looks of it he isn't giving you any play. That has to sting, right? So you hiss and spit at me, but now that we both know where the claws and crazy are coming from, we can be honest with each other. You are starving for it. I'm Stefan Walker. I don't chase any woman who doesn't enjoy the hunt—and you are made for it. As consolation prizes go, I'm a lottery win. Now, open the door and let's use our free time for something way more fun than the snowboarding."

"No."

Stefan laughed. "I was voted the number one celebrity women wanted to get trapped in an elevator with for a quickie—three years in a row! I'm offering you a guilt-free ride here, princess, so stop pretending that you aren't aching to jump in the saddle.

You want a rough ride? Because we can do that, too. Let's see if you can still tell me no when I show you how good this can be."

Lilly blinked twice. It wasn't a question of being in danger. If she confronted him, called hotel security or allowed things to spin out of control, it was a wrinkle in her already wrinkled weekend she couldn't afford. Destroying him was so tempting she had to swallow hard to suppress a smile at the delicious thrill the notion evoked—but again, timing was everything.

Hell hath no fury...like a demon who isn't in the mood for Mr. Stefan Walker!

Although the rub was that he was a human being outside of her mission's perimeters. He had free will and he also had the protections warranted by the Corporation against random acts by Field Agents. Just because she had a hall pass, didn't mean she could strike out in any direction she wished even when a certain human male was begging for demonic retribution.

It was a coin toss and Lillith didn't like the idea that she would lose either way.

"I must have missed that magazine poll. But before you say anything else," Lilly paused to hold up her phone. "You might want to peruse my phone's contact list, Mr. Walker. That producer who is here this weekend is only one of a dozen names you'll recognize and you'll see about twenty more that you'd have sold your left testicle to have a good word put in for you. It's billions of dollars of entertainment heavyweights in the palm of my hand. But, what do you care? You want to play thick-headed villain, force me to open the door and play out your latest rape fantasies? You want to ignore a woman who has refused you publicly and privately as politely as she can? You want to pretend this doesn't end violently and with your career so far down a death-spiral that Webster's doesn't put your picture next to the word for self-destructing narcissistic idiots? I'm happy to oblige you." Lilly held up the phone a little higher. "Or do you want to gamble that I didn't hit 'record' about thirty seconds ago so that this delightful exchange won't become evidence in the charges I will be forced to file after the assault?"

"That's bullsh—" He stopped himself, dropping his arm and eyeing her warily. "You're bluffing."

Lilly touched the button and Stefan's recorded voice rang out. "*You want a rough ride? Because we can do that, too.*"

"It's called flirting! No one's assaulting anybody! You...give me that phone!" He snatched the phone away from her only to have it vanish from his hands. "What the hell!?"

Lilly took one step back. "Forget the phone. Walk away and I'll never mention to another living soul what an ass you are. Your secrets are safe with me. But if you so much as twitch in my direction again, the hotel security cameras will collaborate my testimony as you chase me screaming down these halls…"

"I'm not going to chase you screaming down these halls!"

"Not yet. But you're just stupid enough to act on cue when the moment comes and hit your mark."

"You are a bitch."

Lillith looked at him, a sweet innocent smile on her face as she waited for him to either 'fish or cut bait'.

At last, he turned on his heels and stomped off toward the elevators. Lilly watched his retreat, more than a little disappointed in the man. Downstairs he'd seemed harmless and she'd actually had him on her mental chessboard as a working possibility to make Jackson jealous but now—it was another setback. Stefan was too erratic to use.

But not too crazy to escape getting a black flag in my report once this mission is over.

I see a Take-Down in his pathetic future…

"But not by me!" She fumbled with her card key with numb hands, furious at their trembling. Once safely inside, Lilly checked her phone to comfort herself with the familiar lines of Ben's report and ignored the flat taste of copper-bile that rose in her throat as she accepted how close she'd come to disaster.

"Oh, well. Can't cry over spilt milk." Lilly pulled out an outfit for her next change and began to run a hot bath to recover her equilibrium. But before the mirrors were steamed, she changed her mind and twisted the knobs off to fire up an ice cold shower.

"No more heat, Temptress."

Time to play it cool.

**

Benjamin's hands froze over his keyboard as he absorbed that the voice he was overhearing in the corridor outside his cubicle was none other than the Acting Regent of Hell himself—and that a very unhappy Asmodeus was with him.

"I will pull her from the mission," Asmodeus growled. "If this blasted mortal is so important that you're hovering then we should be better prepared and make a better run at him. Surely Upper Management would want a clean and quick destruction of this man rather than this blind fumbling they force us to with empty files and no reconnaissance to—"

"No." Malcolm cut him off firmly without raising his voice.

Both demons were talking on their way to Asmodeus' office, so Ben leaned over in his chair to try to hear what he could until he was precariously balanced with his ear against the hollow cubicle's wall.

"No?" Asmodeus' steps slowed in shock just a few feet away, unknowingly benefitting Ben's eavesdropping efforts. "I despise being told no."

"Who doesn't?" Malcolm countered, his tone unruffled. "If I am hovering, then I will cease the practice if it unsettles you so much but the mission is important—more important than I am authorized to tell you. However Lillith stays in the field as it has been made clear by Upper Management that they wish her to personally see this through."

"Ridiculous! One Temptress is like any other and what do they care if one useless piece of—"

"Insubordination."

One word. One icy word that held chasms of disapproval, threat and repercussions as the Regent stood silently to allow the word's impact to settle against Asmodeus' skin.

"No insubordination was intended," Asmodeus' voice was even, emotionless.

"See that it doesn't happen again. Intentional or not, I will not overlook it again."

Ben swallowed hard as the silence stretched out until he was sure the only remedy was the sound of a door slamming—or someone getting their neck snapped.

"What in the freakish twists of time are you doing, Benjamin?"

Ben righted himself by pin-wheeling his arms as he jumped up from his seat, immediately aware that he'd been so intent on trying to listen to his boss's conversation that his screensaver had come on to make it look like he'd either been napping or making an intense study of rainbow colored raindrops. "I was lost in thought, Dread Lord."

"Lost. In thought." Asmodeus stood in the cubicle's open entryway and repeated the phrase, fracturing it as if to demonstrate that he was not familiar with the concept.

"Apologies." He meant to say more but his mouth went dry. *I told her it was tense? I bet men in missile silos running blind drills are more relaxed.* "May I help you, sir?"

"Is the Temptress checking in regularly?"

Benjamin nodded. "Lilly is very reliable."

"How did she sound when last you spoke?" Asmodeus pressed. "Is she progressing?"

"She sounded confident and completely relaxed. I think it will be a Take Down for the ages. Get the confetti cannon ready!" Ben forced himself to keep a straight face, completely aware that he had oversold it a little too brightly.

Asmodeus' eyes squinted, a threatening focus that left no room for doubt. The Demonic Prince of Lust was *not* in the mood to play. "If you put that nonsense about confetti into the official reports, I will kill you and consume you. Understood?"

Benjamin nodded not trusting his voice. He dropped his gaze and realized that his screensaver had changed to a montage of kitten photos while they'd talked. *Oh, yeah. I'm all about impressing the powers that be...*

"I want a victory, Benjamin. I want to demonstrate that this department can accomplish any mission that it is assigned. I want shock and awe, Benjamin, to make Heaven, Inc. marvel at our skills." Asmodeus leaned over with a chilling smile on his lips. "I want to show Upper Management how it is done when Asmodeus is in command."

Ben hoped that none of his thoughts were visible in his face.

Okay. Time to have the demigod's meds checked...

"Absolutely. One for the ages."

Asmodeus left without another word and Benjamin had to visually check his pants to ensure that they were still miraculously dry.

Chapter Seven

"The city where Snows Metro Community Hospital resides is as far from real snow as you can get. Or at least, any snow you'd want a kid to play in. It sits in a rough inner-city neighborhood and up until a decade ago it was an outdated and forgotten small medical center offering sub-standard care and limping along to serve the poorest of the poor. But the doctors and nurses knew there was a need and they never gave up. They dreamt of more for their patients and a better life for all."

Jackson Kent was reading from his notes, but he hardly needed them. The topic was as dear to him as any and his passion for the project gave him confidence to address the crowded room. "As Snows has been rejuvenated, so has the neighborhood around it. Community programs have had a huge impact and I'm proud to be a part of that change and to see the Snow Angel Foundation blossom from our humble start with makeshift volunteer support services for cancer patients to what it's become today."

Applause broke out but he held up his hands, anxious that this didn't become a "hooray for Jackson Kent" moment. "I started Snow Angels because alone, I wasn't going to make a dent. But I swallowed my pride, raised my hand and discovered that angels come in all shapes and sizes. Thank goodness!"

"Tonight's the Fire Ball, a terrible name, I know… sorry, folks. I'll do better next time and see if I can't hire some professionals to get me out of trouble but I look forward to seeing all of you in your finest and fieriest! And of course, ahead of that we have a great afternoon of skiing and activities for all of you, including the ice sculpture show on the outdoor verandah and inside, the art gallery of the original works you'll be bidding on at the silent auction tomorrow night. Please take a look at the incredible pieces we've gathered and I'm begging you—I know, it's not pretty to ask you outright, but please open those wallets and bid generously for these one of a kind works of art. And yes, the rumors are true. Hidden in the gallery in plain sight is the ugliest painting ever created by yours truly on a dare, so bids on that one will be taken as payment for its immediate destruction to prevent it from seeing daylight. Save the world and buy my finger painting of my favorite wide receiver!"

The laughter in the room was just what he was hoping for and Jackson relaxed. "Seriously, if you buy my world's ugliest artwork, I'll throw in tickets for next year's Super Bowl to sweeten the pot!"

Several guests began to whoop and yell their support, the excitement over the tickets catching throughout the room.

Laurel stepped up to his elbow and Jackson read her note quickly, then amended his speech. "And yes, that's even if my team isn't in it…"

Jackson tucked the paper in his pocket and continued, trying not to openly scan the room for the one face he'd wanted to see the most. "Tomorrow's the big fun heart of our event with our Children's Silly Skis Tournament. The adult pros will be competing alongside some wonderful young amateurs for medals and prize money but I think no one in this room is unaware of the real winners. The sponsors, the press coverage, all of it…you….you've made every child who comes to Snows Metro Community Hospital and every family who needs hope and support—you've made them winners this weekend!"

Applause exploded again across the large hall and many people were dabbing at their eyes.

It's a good sign. But let's cross our fingers!

Jackson signaled the AV crew to begin dimming the lights and cued them to begin the video. "But you don't need to hear it from me. Here. Here's what you've done, what you are doing and here is what victory looks like…"

He stepped back and a huge blank screen unfurled behind him just as the lights dimmed and the video began just as he spotted her near the back of the room. Relief flooded through him, irrational and sweet, and Jackson had to fight not to jog down the steps of the stage to get to her side.

Lilly's breath caught in her throat. Children. Eyes like innocent mirrors that reflected all the hope and need of the world gazed out from hospital beds. Bald heads and tubes jarred the senses but their beauty was undeniable. Sweet voices spoke out not making whining pleas or to complain but with giggles and gentle smiles they thanked strangers that they could not see for simple gifts, for toys and letting mommy stay in their new room during treatment. For dress ups and story times. For the new addition of a disco ball in the physical therapy room that makes them smile.

The camera caught a few parents, anchoring the images of hospital equipment and terrifying technology hidden by bright colors and clever screens and the staff's efforts to make it all less frightening for these youngest warriors battling for their lives. Giraffes held drip lines and a purple rhinoceros wearing tennis shoes balanced atop a heart monitor.

Lilly watched it all, enrapt and amazed. A temptress knew the workings and worst of the human heart and was all too familiar with the wastes of pleasure when a soul became selfish and blind. But this…this was new ground. Because she instinctively knew who the amateur cameraman was…the way the children were looking up at their photographer…the way every single one of them lit up when he laughed at their antics.

Jackson Kent.

This wasn't a remote project. He was in it.

Heart and soul.

A little boy on the screen wearing his hero's football jersey winked mischievously and then blew a kiss that made her knees go weak. "I'm growing every day! See you in spring training!"

Jackson's voice was heard off camera at last, confirming her suspicions. "You gonna put me on the bench, Max?"

"Yup! Just watch me!" Max giggled and lifted his arms to flex his muscles. "I'm the man!"

"Say thank you to the contributors, Max," Jackson's whisper was barely audible.

Max grinned and looked into the camera. "Thank you, contributors!" he yodeled then tipped his head as if to try to peek at the man behind the lens. "Don't worry. You can be my backup quarterback, okay? I'll put in a good word for you with the coach."

"Thanks, Max."

The video ended with a view of the nursing staff at their station, doctors and technicians all waving at the camera before the screen retreated up into the ceiling. The audience thundered with applause and emotional cries of approval, the atmosphere suddenly electric. Jackson shook his head and pressed a hand over his eyes. "Oh, God. I guess you've met my replacement."

He had to wait several minutes for them to quiet down just enough for him to continue. "You. You made Max's life better. All of the children. Once we have that family center, we take the pressure off all those parents who worry about the expenses of their stays, about being close to their babies when their kids need them most—it's huge. You did that. Not me. You! So I know I'm not a fraction of the cute you just saw and frankly, I'm not a fraction of any of the hard work and heart of it, but I want to make sure you hear it one more time. Thank you! Thank you all!"

They applauded again, a frenzy of tears and happiness.

"Okay! So no excuses! You have a few more chances to push us over the top, friends! Enjoy your lunch and I'll see you out there this afternoon and then tonight at the ball, tomorrow at the ski tournament and the final party and auction; then if you're lucky, I'll let you escape as promised." Jackson gave up as his audience continued to whistle and cheer. He smiled. Max was a charmer but he hadn't quite anticipated how well Max's innocent sporty ambition would go over in a cynical crowd numbed by the usual pitches for charity. He glanced over to see if Lilly had enjoyed it only to realize that she was making what looked like a rushed escape from a burning room.

His smile vanished at the realization.

She was leaving.

Without him.

He put down his mic and leapt off the edge of the stage, sprinting through the tables to catch her before she disappeared. She was through one of the side service doors but she hadn't gone far. She was leaning with her forehead pressed against a floor to ceiling stack of giant boxes holding paper products. Jackson's steps slowed as he took in the realization that this uncarpeted hallway with its bare walls and service items should have been a very unglamorous place but that this woman made it feel as if he'd caught a princess in a dungeon passage.

"Is everything okay?"

She looked up, a flash of surprise and what he almost identified as guilt, before she managed a smile. "I'm fine. It's—a lot to take in. All those children…"

Jackson came closer, anxious to comfort her. "Hey, you wouldn't be human if it didn't affect you, Lilly. No one wants to think about kids being sick." Jackson couldn't stop himself from touching her. She suddenly looked so fragile and lost. He trailed a hand over her shoulder. "But you've done so much for them. There's no need to hide how you feel."

"I'm not—hiding." Lilly straightened but didn't pull away from him. "I just don't want to melt into a puddle of goo and spoil the incredible illusion of perfection I had going." She grimaced, "Well, maybe not perfection considering that stupid front door, or the misstep of overbidding for you at the auction so that you'd make a vow of celibacy, or… Never mind. I'm not crying. I'm a woman overwhelmed with sexual frustration, that's all. Got it?"

"Oh, I got it."

"I've been in a cold shower since breakfast, Kent. At this rate, I'll have pneumonia by Sunday." She tipped her face up to his, her eyes still filled with tears. "So just kiss me already!"

He obliged her without any hesitation but it was the gentlest pass of his lips across hers, not a passionate conquest. She was sweet and soft and he was instantly reminded that Lilly wasn't the only one enduring a bit of sexual frustration. Jackson ended it but pulled her against his chest to hold her in his arms.

"You have a big heart, Lilly."

She shook her head. "I don't. Don't say that. I'm terrible. And I do not cry over…babies."

"No?" Jackson lifted his fingertips to gently capture the clear crystal streaks of her tears before it dripped off her cheek. "Your eyes are leaking, terrible lady."

"W-what?" Lilly started to step back and ran into the barrier of the boxes. "That isn't…excuse me, Mr. Kent. I…need…a tissue."

Jackson felt quickly in his jacket pockets and realized he was about to come up short in the knightly department of princess rescue. That is, until he remembered the labels on the boxes behind her. He was tall enough to reach the highest one, crack the top and retrieve an industrial box of tissues with a flourish. "Tissue."

Lilly pulled three from the top and he frowned as he realized that her hands were shaking. "You get extra points for that one. Now, I'll just…" This time she stepped away from the wall, a woman who now had her bearings. "Go powder my nose upstairs and take another ice bath."

"Lilly."

She began to walk away and then suddenly stopped and turned back to face him. "How much time do you spend at that hospital, Jackson?"

The question was so unexpected, he wasn't sure how many seconds he lost composing his thoughts. "The season's over and…I have more free time for a while."

"How much time do you spend at that hospital?"

Jackson wasn't sure why he felt defensive but there was something in her eyes. Something desperate and raw that demanded the truth. "Whenever I'm not on the road, I try to stop in. My mom still lives in that neighborhood. So…a lot of time, I guess."

"My God. That hospital. It's like your family, isn't it?"

He nodded. "Yes. But this is not a bad thing. Why do I get the feeling I just admitted to an addiction to strip clubs?"

"Do you have an addiction to strip clubs?" she asked more brightly.

"No! Lilly! What is this about?"

"I…don't know yet. I'm still trying to…" Lilly let out a long slow breath. "You are an impossibly good man, Mr. Jackson Kent."

Jackson smiled. "I don't think impossible is the word you're looking for, Lilly."

"What word would you use?"

Jackson shrugged his shoulders. "Let's stick with 'o' and say, ordinary. I might wish for something with bells and whistles but at the end of the day, I'm ordinary with a capital 'O', Lilly."

"Nope." The tears started anew and the look of shock and horror on her face only made it worse. "You're not even close, Mr. Kent."

She ran from him cutting through another doorway into the labyrinth and Jackson was left to blink, a man amazed.

Lilly reached the sanctuary of her room and locked the door with a frustrated sigh. *What the Hell was going on?*
Instead of sharpening her claws, she was losing every hard edge she had—and crying? *Crying?!* It was ridiculous. She should have been climbing him like a tree in that hallway, dropping his pants and getting him into every compromising position she could manage with the aid of six boxes of tissues and toilet paper so that the first hotel staffer with a camera phone could see about securing their retirement with tabloid dollars. It might not have been the most solid finish, but it would have been something.
Instead she'd ran.
Demons do not cry.
A Temptress is many things. But coward is generally not on the list. They are also not known to be sentimental, emotional messes who cling to a man and find themselves the victims of desire. They served it up. They did not crave. They did not long for a man's touch out of his presence. They did not consider one man above another or start to entertain failure. They did not miss the mark. They did not stutter, stumble or fall behind.
And above all things, they did *not* cry.
Her tears rattled her more than she wanted to admit. Every exchange with Jackson was affecting her more. Which meant some clock she wasn't previously aware of was in motion. Her target was proving to be more dangerous than she'd imagined possible. Jackson Kent, ordinary mortal man, was tearing through her internal defenses like wet tissue paper.
If this keeps up, I'll go soft by Monday.
Soft was not acceptable. Demons who lost their edge tended to disappear from the building and the rumors of their ends were the stuff of nightmares.
She sighed and began to pace the room. Demons prided themselves on their self-control. Tears. Tears were for addle-headed fools and angels. It was a running joke in the halls of Hades Enterprises that Angels were notorious for weeping at every rainbow and sunset, and the speculation of what maudlin gifts they exchanged at their office white elephant parties was a vast source of humorous demonic speculation.
Lilly snorted in disgust at the awkward terror of getting a monogrammed tissue box holder from her boss on her return to the office.
"When Hell freezes over!" she proclaimed as her phone signaled an inbound text.
Lilly opened it to see that Ben had already completed a full report. She uploaded it and anxiously scanned the data only to have her disbelief and confusion deepen at every revelation of the man's goodness.
Jackson Kent was a gifted businessman whose investments were solid and very profitable. He led a comfortable life but beyond a great apartment and tasteful wardrobe, he'd taken on none of the trappings of ostentation. No entourage when he traveled. One personal assistant and accountant. One lawyer and the obligatory sports agent behind the scenes. Lillith's disbelief and confusion only deepened at every detailed non-revelation.
The accountant was his college roommate and best friend and his lawyer was the daughter of his favorite high school coach. The man was incredibly loyal to his roots.

He wrote thank you notes to associates and fans and still sent letters to his fifth grade math teacher every year on the first day of school to wish her luck.

He's a walking Norman Rockwell!

No car collections or million dollar private home theater, no private plane or helicopter and apparently he was the proud owner of a city transit pass. Most reported bad habit: Over-tipping.

Over-tipping? That's the only thing popping up?

The demon who can predict a mortal's every choice at a thousand item all-you-can-eat buffet after scanning their grocery receipts…just admitted he has No Idea what makes Jackson Kent tick and that Hell's IT department was coming up empty-handed.

Even her idea that the Snow Angel connections might be a source of trouble for Jackson had turned up only more glowing praise. The hospital board was beyond normal. Retired physicians, veteran CEO's and professional businessmen. No scandal was evident and Jackson's involvement was completely legitimate. No affairs. Nothing dirty. The money was clean, accounted for and conservatively invested to protect the charitable foundation's assets—and not put into anything that he had any personal holdings in to avoid a conflict of interest.

The only surprise in the entire report was that Jackson Kent's mother still worked despite his generosity giving her the option to retire on some balmy tropical island in luxury. Mrs. Kent worked as a dental hygienist at Snows Metro Community Hospital in the adult oncology ward and volunteered to work with the pediatric departments to help younger patients struggling with the side-effects of their treatments and the loss of their smiles. Ben had even included an article from some medical publication on how dental health was often forgotten in life and death struggles but how neglect could lead to serious infections and setbacks for patients.

TMI, Ben. Oh, man! He's so desperate to show me he tried that he put a list of the best floss for kids in here. Right…as if that bit of trivia is going to help!

The final typed note in Ben's report made her knees go numb.

"Mission reconfirmed as Priority Alpha Rating by Corporate."

Lilly put the phone down and then pressed the heels of her hands against her eyes. "Time to get a grip, girl."

Okay. His mom is a saint cleaning people's teeth and helping sick people. Clearly, the boy comes by his propensity to wear a cape somewhat naturally. Perhaps having a mom for a saint has forced him to try to play the role…

Except if he was playing a role by rote, he was doing it with incredible dedication and more convincingly than any award-winning actor. She'd seen enough miserable men going through the motions of lives they didn't want, to spot the syndrome. Jackson didn't give any signs of being trapped but Lilly grasped at the tenuous theory with stubborn desperation. She headed for the bathroom and began to draw a nice hot bath to help her sort things out.

She'd yet to meet a good boy who didn't secretly wish to be a very bad man behind closed doors, and she'd be damned if she'd make the mistake of missing such an obvious hook.

"He wants me."

The words were vaguely reassuring. In just a few hours, the Fire Ball was on the schedule and if ever a woman were going to pull out a red dress and see if she couldn't heat things up, the event seemed tailor made for a seduction of epic proportions.

Lillith studied her reflection before the steam hid it from her.

"No more of this sweet nonsense. Tonight, we go back to basics, Mr. Kent, and if there's a bad boy hiding in there somewhere, you better get ready to cut him loose."

Even if I have to drag him out kicking and screaming...those pants are off!

**

Jackson had stopped himself from chasing her. He didn't want to be the guy who was constantly running after her only to end up mauling her or making her cry. His phone buzzed with an emotionless persistence that made him growl in frustration. It was Laurel and he answered it quickly.

"Kent here."

"Okay. The construction teams are working hard on the set-ups for tomorrow and I need you to come walk it with me. There's a question about the lay-out and a few surprise piles of snow we didn't expect." She was all business. "It's free time for the attendees, so I think it's now or never before you get ready for tonight."

"I hear you. Sounds like it's now." Jackson cast one last look at the doors that Lilly had gone through and sighed. *That is a woman who needs a little space and I think leaving the building is the only way to force myself to give it to her. Otherwise I'm that cliché guy pounding on her hotel room door...* "I'm on my way. I'll meet you in the lobby by the registration desk and we'll walk out from there."

"Check." Laurel hung up efficiently and without a lot of ceremony.

The behind the scenes maelstrom was gearing up to full capacity. She touched base with the tech team handling all the audio-video for the weekend and handed over a list of songs she did *not* want to hear at the Fire Ball that night.

"One whiff of the Macarena and I'll skin someone alive," she grumbled as the D.J. took the list.

"You sure?" he asked dryly. "It gets 'em on the floor."

Before she could reply, he winked to make sure she was in on the joke and Laurel forced herself to smile on an exhale. Her mood hadn't improved since breakfast, though the success of the lunchtime presentation felt like a solid hurdle to clear. Jackson had nixed the heartstrings soundtrack she'd suggested during his speech but his instincts had proven him right.

Less was more, though she wasn't completely convinced that more wasn't also an option to get to "more".

Laurel headed toward the lobby's registration desk, determined to be the first one there. She was and then happily noted that when Jackson arrived he did not have a certain sexy shadow trailing behind him.

The mystery of Miss Lillith Fields wasn't fading and no matter what Jackson said, Laurel didn't believe in benevolent sirens that dropped out of the blue. So far, she'd kept him busy and out of harm's way and if everything went according to plan, Jackson would have time to sit down with Miss Fields right after the event closer on Sunday morning—and not a minute before then.

The small team assembled and everyone put on their coats before heading out. Laurel trailed Jackson, taking notes and highlighting all decisions and action-items the men created as they walked and talked.

Jackson was a born leader, collaborative and calm, putting all of them at ease even on the eve of such a huge undertaking. Apparently, this was the first year the Snow Angels Foundation was incorporating the ski tournament into their efforts and the potential success of it was daunting. They'd sold out every ticket available to the public, so the pressure was tremendous not to disappoint.

Laurel admired the man's mind and chastised herself more than once for admiring a bit more of his backside and the shape of his shoulders as she followed in his footsteps.

Damn it. This is ridiculous. And if Miss Fields hadn't made me bring up that stupid magazine ad, I wouldn't be having such a hard time with my—imagination!

The walk-thru was extensive and by the time they were nearly done, the sun had started to set and she could see his attention wandering back to the hotel as he glanced up at the upper floors of the hotel as if to catch a glimpse of his lovely Lilly.

Laurel sighed. "The reporter from the Post wanted to get a picture of you with your painting before things get rolling."

Jackson grimaced. "I'm not sure I want to be immortalized with that thing. I mean…don't get me wrong! I was really trying to come up with a decent portrait of Wayne but if Picasso and Dali got in a food fight with a spider monkey, it would still look better than that thing."

"Exactly! That's the humorous point of it, right? And the football tickets were a stroke of genius, if I can say so." Laurel held up her tablet. "So that's a yes to the Post? It would certainly raise the profile of the event if it goes viral…"

He took the bait and nodded consent. "Okay. No sense in me getting shy about it now."

"If you'll change, we'll get it out of the way next so that you'll still have time to get set for tonight."

"I was going to see if Miss Fields wanted to walk through the gallery before the Ball."

"No go. Maybe you can slip away once it gets going but the pre-party reception with the board members and annual donors was moved back onto the schedule, remember?" Laurel said, a vague sense of victory seeping into her spine. "You okayed that this morning."

"I did?" Jackson ran a hand through his hair. "Well, thank God someone's taking notes then. But if you can't find me later at the Fire Ball, I'd appreciate it if you didn't look too hard, Miss Marsh."

"I'm not making any promises, sir." Laurel smiled. "But I'll do my best to keep the wolves at bay."

"You rock," he said, a man assured even if she had been deliberately vague.

They parted ways from the elevators as she stepped off to head to her room to change clothes for the night. Not that it would be much of a transformation. Every gown she'd brought was a different colored clone of the same bridesmaid's dress.

Laurel set aside her notes from the afternoon and opened her closet to eye her choices. The best assistants were known for blending quietly into the background but

Laurel wasn't sure she was happy disappearing into the wallpaper anymore. Not that she had any illusions of competing with Miss Fields but she wasn't sure what she wanted.

Maybe just to keep Jackson Kent's mind on his charitable foundation and on track for protecting his amazing reputation.

He wanted to spend as much of his spare time as possible with Miss Fields.

Laurel was simply determined that he had no spare time.

She'd been surprised that Lilly had even shown up for the luncheon presentation since she'd already made her sizable donation but there was no telling when trouble would strike. As far as Laurel was concerned, tonight was the most dangerous when it came to Miss Fields and any entanglements with Jackson. Tomorrow, the ski tournament and evening events would swallow up every spare second the man had. But tonight once the music started, he was on his own and there wasn't a clipboard or tablet on the planet with the power to distract him from a woman like Lilly Fields.

Unless, Lilly herself got distracted by something or someone.

Laurel pulled out her red dress and quickly rushed through her preparations.

"I promised him I'd keep the wolves at bay," she told her reflection. "But if you ask me, Miss Lillith Fields looks a heck of a lot like a werewolf from where I'm standing so—let the games begin."

Chapter Eight

Once again, Lilly made her sultry entrance into the hotel's ballroom, but this time she was ready for anything. She spotted a few familiar faces but made no effort to engage with anyone. The last thing she wanted was another public round with Stefan or even the awkward appearance of a well-intentioned chaperone by way of Mrs. Rickett. Instead, she picked up a glass of champagne and made a circuit of the room. Red and black banners proclaimed the Fire Ball's color themes and she began to smile. The man's passion for his charity didn't gift him with extensive creative powers.

"What's so funny?" Jackson asked as he took her elbow.

"I was just grateful you didn't focus on the angel part of the Snow Angel Foundation. I don't think I can carry off wings." Lilly deliberately shifted her hips to show off the red silk fall of her gown and the way it clung to her body. "Red is my signature color."

"It certainly is." Jackson's look was one of heated approval and raw appreciation. "But I'm going to disagree about the wings. I think you'd put a few supermodels to shame strutting around with—"

"I don't do runway." Lilly pressed her palm against his heart. "Who needs an audience when there's only one man's attention I want?"

"Dance with me."

She started to nod but then caught wind of the energy around them and the audience she'd just decried was beginning to form. Apparently it was going to take more than a cold shower and a deflection spell to dampen the glow coming off them both. "Mr. Kent, if you wanted to avoid a scandal then maybe we should skip the dance floor."

Jackson looked behind him and then laughed. "Whoops!"

He nodded at a few familiar faces and politely led her away from the crowd. "So much for that illusion I had about stealing a few low key moments away before things got crazy."

"I do love your optimism." Lillith fell into step next to him, enjoying the way he chivalrously shifted to make sure that she wasn't jostled by the crowd. "Not due for any speeches tonight? No presentations to make?"

"Not one. Tonight is for socializing before the main event tomorrow."

"The bachelor auction wasn't the main event?"

He laughed. "It wasn't *supposed* to be but it might be tough to top."

Lilly pursed her lips into a very pretty pout. "Does that mean you aren't even going to try?"

"Oh, I'll never stop trying to impress you, Miss Fields." He covered her hand with his own and then ferried her outside onto the ballroom's verandah. The air was crisp and invigoratingly cold but it wasn't an entirely uncomfortable change after the pressing heat of the large crowded party.

Besides even if she'd wished to protest her abrupt exposure to the elements, Lillith forgot to complain. The night was clear and the sky was a canopy of infinite diamonds without a moon to compete for attention and the balcony had been transformed into a magical wintry scene with ice sculptures set out in a labyrinth of breathtaking art in the form of ice castles and dragons. Each piece was lit from within in a different hue and Lilly gasped at the illusion of permanence and the strange sensation of walking through a virtual garden of snow and ice.

"I know you probably saw them in the daylight this afternoon, but I think at night, they're even more spectacular, wouldn't you agree?" he asked. He took off his jacket without a word and put it around her shoulders. "It was a splurge but the hotel will set them out around the grounds after the event so in a way, we get to leave them as a parting gift to all the locals for their support."

"It's lovely! But it makes me a little sad," she said.

"Sad? Sad wasn't on the docket. Where did we take a left turn into sad?"

Lillith tipped her head up to study a fairy tale tower with a tiny Rapunzel lowering a rope of snowflakes to the balcony's floor. "It's beautiful but it won't last. I want it to last." She looked back to Jackson, savoring the echoes of his body heat in the lining of his jacket. "I want *all* of it to last."

He slid his hands around her waist, drawing her close and adding to the tendrils of warmth that snaked up her spine.

"I'd see about investing in refrigeration systems and build a house filled with ice sculptures if it meant keeping you happy, Lilly."

"I hate the cold."

Every seductive power she possessed unfurled as she pressed herself against him, an open invitation that had nothing to do with further conversation. Lips parted, she held nothing back and Jackson proved human after all.

He kissed her, a thorough, commanding and passionate kiss that made her knees feel weak and she eagerly responded to the sexual fires he ignited inside of her. The joy of finally having him without tears or hiccups or the cloud of any disasters added a giddy quality to her sighs. She was a Temptress again, her confidence restored, but more amazingly, the strength of her need for Jackson was a force all its own. Her kisses had lost their practiced precision and instead, Lilly was swept along in every caress and contact of his skin to hers. She'd have accused him of using tricks to provoke her senses but she knew better.

He was a man—and that was all the magic he needed.

This time she did more than melt in sweet surrender. She was all in.

The tables turned and the creature used to dishing out teasing tastes of lust to her unwitting victims was transformed into a woman swept up away with her body's hunger for his. She cursed the tight mermaid style of her skirt, wishing she'd opted for something with a slit so that she could wrap her legs around the man's waist and achieve wicked things with the use of the nearest table or the balcony's railings.

Lillith was past worry about modesty and the role of a sweet philanthropist.

She was in a crush of emotion she couldn't identify.

It was only when they shifted over to lean against an ornate ice sculpture of Poseidon and his sea foam horses that reality breeched her defenses and robbed her of victory by jolting Jackson into an icy awakening.

"We're going to melt these statues, Miss Fields. And as great as that sounds, I think the steam is going to give us away…"

"Ice is made to melt," she whispered before gently nipping at his earlobe and doing her very best to initiate another scorching round. "And I was made to kiss you, Jackson Kent."

"I like the way *that* sounds. Damn it, who am I kidding?" Jackson smiled as he pulled her back into his arms. "I love the way that sounds!"

"Let's go upstairs, Jackson. Enough ice and snow. Take me to bed and let's start a fire…"

"Monday."

"W-what?"

"We have to wait until Monday, Lilly. Once this weekend is over and we're out of the eye of the press, then there's nothing to spoil it. And Lilly? I don't want anything to spoil this."

"That's your Hail Mary? Wait until Monday?!"

"What's the rush? I'm not going anywhere and believe it or not, I'm not some stereotypical jock pushing to muscle you into my bed at the first opportunity. You're a woman worth waiting for, Lilly. Hell, I've already waited a lifetime for the right woman to come along, so what's a couple of days more?"

"You're serious."

"Lilly, sleeping with you isn't some kind of end game or goal for me. It'll happen, no question," he paused to get the pace of his breathing under control as his imagination tried to kickstart the process. "But I want the whole package. I want all of you, in bed and out of it." He winced. "I know it's a little fast to say…I don't want to scare you off, Lilly. I just want to reassure you that I'm not interested in a hit and run. That's all."

"That's so sweet of you." Lilly's grip tightened on his arms. "But I'm not scared. If you were any more sincere, I'm struggling to picture it. So, no worries about rushing things. I trust you completely. Rush all you want. Let me rephrase that. I want you to rush."

Jackson laughed. "Lilly! You are so funny! Thank you for being so sweet about this."

Lilly blinked. *Sweet? Who the Hell was being sweet?*

Her desire for him was simmering in a tight grind of heat that was spreading through her body and denying her brain much needed oxygen—and the man was talking about Mondays and packages? The Temptress tipped her head to one side and accepted that a temper tantrum was going to lose more than it gained in this instance, so if 'sweet' was all she had at hand, then so be it.

"I'm not the kind of girl who…" Lilly teased her lower lip with her teeth, a blend of a shy pout and a sexual bombshell. "This is new to me, Jackson. I don't melt all over a man and beg him to throw me over his shoulders and carry me away but ever since I saw you in the lobby, I…haven't been myself."

"Who'd you become?" he asked playfully.

"Before my glorious entrance into this hotel, I was very scary. I was a force to be reckoned with and I was not interested in much beyond the tip of my fingers."

"Really?" Jackson wry smile betrayed his disbelief. "A real dragon lady, huh?"

"Yes!" Lilly nodded. "That's a great way to put it, Jackson."

"Okay, that was *before*. Who are you now?"

"I don't know. You've scrambled my circuits and I've turned into cannon fodder. I've turned into a woman who doesn't keep what she wants at arm's length. A woman who isn't afraid. You've made me soft and clingy and…" Lilly's breath caught in her throat. "I'm on dangerous ground, Jackson Kent."

He took her hands into his, a tender look in his eyes. "Not even close. You're never in danger when you're with me, Lilly."

She squeezed his fingers, a strange desperation seizing her. "Great. Let's get naked, Jackson. Please. I don't want to wait. I need to get past this feeling."

"Whoa!"

Lilly watched in amazement as Jackson's demeanor shifted from interest to raw concern.

"Lilly, meeting someone fantastic and getting to know them is supposed to be the best part. If you want to run past it, then I'm worried. Sex is a lot of things but a simplifier of problems or a fast move to erase pain, I don't think it's ever worked out that way. This is you and me."

"You and me," she repeated in a wary whisper. The broken wing ploy was sure fire and a man's ego generally took over at the vague suggestion that the emergency miracle cure to all her ills could be found in his manly parts. "Wow."

"You're so gorgeous, Lilly. I hate to think of all the men who never bothered to look beyond the surface and who would be dragging you into the elevators right about now… You deserve better."

"Brace yourself, Kent. You can't say things like that and look at me like a goddess and expect me to stop asking you to drop your pants. In fact, I'd guess that's a bit of an accelerant, wouldn't you, Casanova?"

"My bad. Brace yourself, Fields. I intend to say a lot of nice things to you before I drop my pants."

It was her turn to laugh and Lilly gave in to the insanity of the debate. "Great. It's the weirdest truce in the history of relationships."

"Maybe. But if it's with you, then I'm happy."

"Jackson. How are…you possible? I mean, I've never met any other man like you and I'm starting to wonder where you come from."

"I'm possible because of my mom." He grimaced. "That didn't sound very clever, did it?"

"Go on."

"I guess everyone has heard the story. Single mom, three jobs, struggling on assistance and putting herself through school to try to make sure her boy had a better life." Jackson's expression took a far off cast as memories flitted through his mind. He dreamily traced the lines of her palm and Lilly quietly waited for him to choose the thread he wished to share. "She raised me alone because her family didn't believe in mixed race marriage and it was hard but I don't remember it being hard. I just remember…"

"Yes?"

"I remember loving her. I remember laughing. I remember how she made me feel important and valued. As if we were superheroes and our one-bedroom apartment was our secret hideout in between missions. We'd talk about our dreams and our goals, and she never mocked me when I told her I was going to be a star athlete or buy her a big house one day." He smiled. "Or build a building that flew."

Jackson shook himself as if recalling his present surroundings. "What I'm saying is that the press always wanted to make it sound like I grew up in filth or clutching rags in the winter, but it wasn't that bad. In any case, whatever dues we paid, I'm glad."

"She made you."

"She did and when I turned ten, we had the talk."

"The talk?" Lilly straightened in surprised interest. "The sex talk?"

"No!" He laughed. "I guess I should come up with a different name for it. It was…this amazing conversation where—everything shifted."

"Shifted how?"

"She told me that I was in charge of what kind of man I became. Just me. She told me that every decision, even the little ones that most people throw away, every choice was part of it. She wanted me to know that I was the architect of what sort of man I would be and if I made a difference in this world, it was all in my hands." Jackson sighed. "It was the most profound empowering pep-talk I have ever heard."

"Isn't everyone in charge of who they are?" she asked.

"Of course they are but they don't seem to know it. They blame their parents or rotten luck or their surroundings or a lousy coach or falling into the wrong crowd or… They look out and see who led them off into the weeds, I think." Jackson pressed his palm to hers, enfolding her fingers with his. "I'm no saint, Lilly. I've made more than my fair share of mistakes but all along, I just try to remember that it's up to me to be the man I want to be. Even if that means failing sometimes, it guarantees I'm not afraid to face my own reflection."

Lilly held her breath. "And your father? What kind of man is he?"

"The public story is that he died before I was born but…" Jackson's expression clouded slightly. "He was a bad guy. He abused my mom and tried to kill her when she was pregnant with me. She left him without even a change of clothes and escaped with her purse and enough money for a bus ticket out of town. I dug a little bit, read a police report and decided that there was nothing there in the past for me but useless pain. He's nothing to me and I am *nothing* like him. That's my choice, Lillith."

"Aren't you worried that your success might draw him out? That he'll try to make some claim?" she asked.

Jackson shook his head. "I don't worry about things I can't control. Life's too short."

"So, self-determination? That's the secret to your success? To you? That's it?"

"That's a lot, isn't it?"

"It must be. Apparently it's enough to make a man—well, to make a Jackson Kent." Lilly blinked. "So much for those stupid theories about you being part of a cult drinking the blood of unicorns."

"Lilly!"

"Sorry, just trying to lighten the mood."

"Okay, Fields. I've had it. I'm opening up like a man on truth serum over here and you haven't so much as hinted at your hometown. Give it up, woman."

Lilly smiled. "Wow. Give it up? My brain just fired up in a very naughty direction when you said that. Sorry."

"You're deliberately trying to sidetrack me."

"Damn right." Lillith arched her back and deliberately took advantage of the setting, completely aware of the way the lit ice sculptures would silhouette her figure, of the way she dazzled his senses and most of all, the way he was entangling every needful thread she possessed. "If you think I'm following that epic tale of your childhood and the triumph of the true love of your mom with some weak milk toast story about a poor little rich girl, you have lost your ever loving mind."

"Aw, come on!"

"No. Don't push it or I'll pop a strap on this dress and stage a wardrobe malfunction that guarantees I get out of this conversation without a single argument on your part." Lilly mockingly underlined the threat by trailing her fingertips up to one spaghetti strap to start to pull it down over the creamy curves of her shoulder. "Don't think I won't."

Jackson held his hands up in surrender. "Okay, you win. You get to save the full bio for tomorrow."

She let go of the strap with a pout. "I'm going to have to get used to your definition of victory, Mr. Kent."

"It's not even the first quarter yet, Lilly. I am not the kind of man to give up easily."

She crossed her arms defensively. "I don't want to hear about your fighting spirit when I'm making a fool of myself and tossing up white flags over here."

"You might be many things but I don't think you're a fool." He caught her elbows. "I...I've never met a woman like you before, Lilly. I'm not saying I don't want you, Lilly. I'm saying the opposite and I'm—"

"Pardon me for interrupting," Laurel said then cleared her throat politely as she made her presence known. "But several members of the board were looking for you...and there's a news crew hoping for additional footage of the party and they need your sign off."

"Damn." Jackson's curse before he turned to return to his duty was spoken in the quietest whisper and only Lilly could hear it, but of all the day's developments, she seized on it as progress. Instead of glaring at Laurel, she found herself smiling at last.

It's the first crack I've seen in my sexy saint's armor, even if it is only a hairline fracture.

Chapter Nine

Saturday dawned like a postcard despite a sleepless night and Lillith decided to make the best use of her time before the tournament started by swinging through the small gallery to look at the art up for auction. Jackson's ugliest painting in the world was easy to spot amidst several gorgeous professionally created pieces worthy of any museum.

It was the worst mash of color she'd ever seen and if Jackson hadn't mentioned it was a portrait of a teammate, she'd have mistaken it for a moose wearing an old-fashioned bathing suit holding a tennis racket.

Max could be the real artist of this particular work...

Except she knew he wasn't. Jackson would never had applied the word 'ugly' to a child's efforts and the signature in the bottom corner of the canvas was his own. It was Jackson Kent's hand and the humble act of exposing his deficiencies added to the man's overall appeal.

The previous evening had ended in a draw but the power of his kisses made her feel as if there'd been progress—and if nothing else, he'd looked positively miserable to end things as they had. She'd composed an upbeat message to Ben that implied that she was on the brink of success. Lilly had wisely omitted any mention of Jackson's gallant 'Hail Mary' to put her off until Monday. She had the day and one more night to finish her mission.

She eyed the bids on the card set out on the table in front of it and smiled. The bidding was very generous and onto a second card as the lure of the championship tickets and the cause overcame the moose's lack of charms.

"It would serve the Corporation right if I made them regret that unlimited budget," she said then laughed.

Lilly fingered the card and considered the pleasure of another jaw dropping play. The bids were anonymous by an attendee's number assigned in their registration packets. A wicked idea coalesced in her mind and Lilly sent a quick text to Ben and received an equally fast reply.

Lilly smiled and wrote down an unbeatable dollar amount.

That should be fun to watch tonight!

A chime on her phone heralded the time to head outside. Most of the crowds were already on the slopes, the charity ski tournament already underway. Lillith sighed and put on the coat she had draped over her arm. She'd chosen a fitting outfit for the day and something appropriate for the weather. Still, cold was cold and snow was an unfamiliar challenge. It was like walking on greased marbles, even with the shoveled paths and plowed areas leading to the bleachers and sidelines along the courses. She was used to her mastery of a sexy sashay in heels across solid flooring but this—this was more like the march of the penguins. She felt like an idiot as she navigated her way through the crowd in a subtle search for Jackson.

Banners for the event were strung over the finish lines and colorful flags fluttered merrily from every post. Children's laughter and the commentary of the race's officials created an uplifting din along with the cheers of the bystanders. The ski lodge's elegant exterior had been transformed into a winter playground for adults and children alike and Lilly would have admired it more if she weren't so distracted by the slick ice and snow under her heels. There was still no sign of Jackson which perversely made her grateful because Lilly was fairly sure she was a few seconds away from an inglorious attempt at doing the splits.

"Enjoying the day, Miss Fields?" Laurel asked pertly, appearing behind her in a shapeless parka with a clip board in hand.

"It's one thrilling moment after another. And you?"

"It's very pleasant although technically I'm on duty until Sunday morning."

Me, too.

"I still don't think it's an excuse not to make the most of things and let your hair down, Miss Marsh."

"No chance of that." Laurel nervously tucked a stray curl behind her ear. "I heard a rumor that you had the one and only Stefan Walker introducing himself to you at breakfast yesterday morning. What a thrill! I think if a movie star like that walked up to me I would faint dead away."

"A rumor? Did his rumor come complete with him crying in the little boy's room afterward? I did have my heart set on someone needing to lure him out of the handicapped stall with a compact mirror and a tabloid magazine."

"No. I'm—You aren't a fan of his?"

Lilly's instincts tingled with a new awareness. Laurel's color was a touch too high and her tone was off. "Are *you*? A fan of Mr. Walker's?"

"No more than any other woman using oxygen," she said. "Right?"

Lilly shook her head slowly. "He is an ass. He's a borderline sociopath and I wouldn't be surprised if he's convicted of rape in the near future."

"Rape? What are you saying? Stefan Walker is…" Laurel's cheeks blazed with her misery. "Oh, God."

Lillith went on relentlessly. "The mystery is that he knew my room number… You don't think the hotel would be so lax as to give out that kind of information, do you? I do make an effort to guard my privacy."

"Oh, God." Laurel dropped her clipboard in the snow and had to kneel to gather her things. "He—seemed so charming. I didn't imagine…"

"Relax. He never got out of the hallway past my doorway, and I doubt he'll make another run at it."

"I thought—he's such a catch and he made it sound like you really liked him! Why would he do that?" Laurel's eyes filled with tears. "I'm so sorry! I thought if you met someone like Mr. Walker, he could distract you from Jackson and—"

Laurel's hand flew to her mouth, stifling her own words.

Lilly sighed, then smiled as she helped Laurel put her clipboard back in order. "I can tell when someone is practiced in evil deeds and you, Miss Laurel Marsh, have no skills in that arena. Seriously, none, so I believe you."

Laurel's eyes widened in shock. "How is it I feel simultaneously relieved and a little hurt by that?"

"The worst schemers always have the best intentions."

"Did he hurt you?" Laurel asked, her expression full of dread. "Did he—"

"Don't worry. I am unbruised and flattered you'd try to send in such a big gun to take me out. But Mr. Walker was no match for my claws and my vengeance is already in play."

"Did you call hotel security? Should I ask him to leave the event?"

"Miss Marsh, trust me. Misunderstandings happen and so long as you didn't slip my room number into anyone else's pockets, I'm happy to let the matter drop. Okay?"

"Why are you being so kind? So forgiving?" Laurel took a step back warily.

Lilly held her breath and decided that for once, honesty might be the best policy. "Because with this secret between us, I know you won't try anything else for fear that I'll tell Jackson. I really wasn't hurt and I think we need a truce, you and I. Wouldn't you agree?"

"Of course!" Laurel pressed her fingertips against one cheek, as if trying to physically hold back the color that was flooding her face. "I think I should get back to work before I…I don't know. I'm so embarrassed," she finished miserably.

"Yes!" Lilly linked her arm with Miss Marsh's, her lifeline to remaining upright. "As part of your agenda, could you help me find Jackson? I seem to have gotten a late start and frankly, I don't know where to begin to look in these crowds."

"Sure. Hold on." Laurel's relief was tangible at being able to return to the business at hand and she whipped out a small walkie-talkie from her pocket. "Marsh here. Has anyone got the 4-1-1 on Mr. Kent?"

There was a brief crackle of static then, "He's over at the war zone."

"Great, thanks!" Laurel replied brightly and put the device away. "It's at the far end over there but I'll take you."

"War zone?" Lilly asked. "Is there a darker aspect to a Silly Skis Tournament I missed?"

"Hardly. You'll see for yourself."

Laurel began to lead her out along all the finish lines where it was smoothest, even if it was also where most of the crowd had gathered to cheer on the finishing competitors. Bleachers were set up for makeshift stands and there was not an empty seat anywhere. A news van was parked at the edge of the event next to a booth where a mock sports desk was set up for children to take turns playing at sports announcer as their parents took photos and videos of the game.

Lilly's grip on Laurel's arm betrayed her bad balance but she was too proud to let go. "I've never understood why anyone thinks risking broken ankles and frozen extremities is a great way to spend their vacations."

"People do more than vacation. They live here."

Lilly's astonished squeak was genuine. "On purpose?"

Laurel laughed. "It's beautiful and once you find your feet, it can be a lot of fun, Miss Fields, year round."

Lilly didn't answer. The mystery of the alluring appeal of winter was beyond her and arguing that when tropical islands existed no other option should be on the table didn't seem wise. Instead she lifted her chin and kept trying to channel more of a sure-footed snow leopard and a bit less of a penguin.

Laurel led her steadily past the snow block obstacle course with igloos and a bubble blower set up to make a friendly blizzard for the tiniest competitors and the rainbow snow tracks created for the tandem ski where professional skiers were towing laughing children either on skis themselves or on sleds in a race that no one seemed to lose. There was even a child-size ski jump set up where everyone cheered as the bravest souls in the junior set landed in a pit of foam blocks.

"Would you like a cup of hot chocolate, Miss Fields?"

Lilly stopped in her tracks. It was a beverage she had never encountered before but at the word 'chocolate', she was an intrigued demon. "Is it good?"

Laurel nodded slowly. "I can't imagine how it couldn't be."

"I'll take one."

The women stopped at a craft service that was set up to provide hot chocolate to all the volunteers and Laurel handed her a steaming paper cup topped with marshmallows. It took one sip for the Temptress to decide that hot chocolate was going on her personal wicked pleasures top ten list. Not only was it delicious but the warmth it evoked internally made her want to giggle. Or…it did until she realized that Laurel was staring at a grown woman gripping her cup and sighing in ecstasy over what was apparently a common beverage.

"It's…really good." Lilly relaxed her hold on the cup but couldn't make herself drop it in the trash.

"Was that your—first hot chocolate?"

Lilly took another sip from her cup and shrugged her shoulders. "And here I thought there was nothing in the vast landscape of human experiences I'd missed. Oh, well. We'd better set about finding Jackson."

"He's bound to be swamped without a minute to spare," Laurel said.

"I won't take up too much of his time. I just wanted to wish him luck on the tournament and make sure he sees me outside at least once." Lilly laughed at her own joke. "Just in case you've been trying to convince him that Stefan Walker isn't the only vampire supporting his charity."

Laurel rolled her eyes. "Please don't say his name again. I can't believe you aren't cringing every time you hear it."

"I never dwell on villains—at least, not until I have to." Lilly gently took her new friend's arm again with her free hand. "Come on, let's go for a trudge!"

Laurel complied and they finally made their way to a clear, flat area set out with a disjointed maze of low walls made out of snow with a flag at its center displaying the Snow Angels' logo. Spectators lined the circular area yelling out names and encouragement but for a few seconds, Lilly couldn't fathom what in the world they were so excited about.

Until she heard Jackson yell, "Lay on!"

Children popped up from makeshift bunkers and snowballs began flying every direction. Squeals of delight from the victims and victors alike rang out and the battle over who could reach the circle's center and capture the flag. It was chaos in hilarious bursts of snowball volleys as warriors cried for more ammo while others made clown-like shows of betraying their allies and more than one snowball landed outside the arena to take out a cheering bystander.

"Oh, the *war zone*," Lillith exclaimed softly. "What fun!"

But where is Jackson?

She didn't want to get too close for fear of taking a hit but the playful struggle was mesmerizing. After just a minute or two, a whistle blew and all the children popped up with their hands over their heads as if to surrender to the referee. The piercing sound helped her locate her quarry at last as she spotted him atop a small ladder on the other side of the mini-arena.

"Okay! That's time! The flag still stands untouched but we're going to give the round to Brian for the most snowball hits and also points to Ashley for the most dramatic fake death ever performed at a snowball fight. Well done!" Jackson clapped and the crowd joined him, even while the king and queen of the last round basked in the glow. Apparently Ashley was a shyer diva than she'd appeared—but Brian puffed up like a rooster on a roofline and Lillith laughed out loud.

Jackson's gaze caught hers and he quickly called out, "We're going to take a five minute rest before the next battle, so all participants please check in with your mom and dad, get some hot chocolate and fortify yourselves! When you hear the whistle, we'll get set to go again! Okay, everybody! Go have fun!"

He climbed down and hurried over to her, his pleasure at seeing her making the moment slightly awkward as Laurel took an invisible step to the left.

"I have to go make sure the services volunteers are covered," Laurel offered. "If you'll excuse me."

"Thanks, Laurel. Let me know if they need anything or if there are any problems," Jackson said though it was clear he was struggling not to stare at Lillith in her cotton candy pink ski clothes and boots with the matching swing coat. "Have John radio to find me."

"Will do, boss," Laurel said and left them alone with a quick, graceful retreat.

"Lilly, what are you wearing?" he asked softly.

"What? This old thing?" Lilly shimmied to show off her figure. "It's pink."

He laughed. "I can see that. You look good enough to eat."

The instant the words came out of his mouth, she watched his color change and knew he'd just detonated an internal cascade of wicked erotic imaginative explosions that underlined her power.

She looked at him through the fluttering veil of her lashes, deliberately throwing a little more fuel on the fire.

"Don't. Lilly. If you only knew the night I just had..."

She opened her mouth to say something provocative in return but Jackson didn't give her time. He kissed her hard enough and thoroughly enough to derail her speech, scramble her wits and make her drop her drink.

Terrible thing to litter. Oh, no. What if that's the worst thing I manage to get the man to do? Make him...litter in a public place...oh...I'll...put it in...the report....later....

His mouth was warm and firm and his tongue tasted of chocolate and marshmallows which made her groan in a hot rush of happiness. She parted her lips even more to deepen the kiss and invite him to take whatever he wished but a wolf-whistle from someone in the crowd ended the embrace abruptly.

Jackson lifted his head to set her gently away, his smile a dreamy look of contented longing. "One more day, Miss Fields. One more."

Lilly bit her lower lip in frustration. "Nonsense. You've kissed me in public in front of hundreds of people. Scandal achieved. Let's throw caution to the winds and find the nearest quiet corner, Kent. What do you say to doing something naughty in the back of that concession stand over there?"

He laughed and put up his hands in a playful show of surrender. "Very funny, Fields."

She crossed her arms with a pout. "Who's being funny?"

Her show of temper had the opposite effect she'd expected and Jackson's amusement only increased. "Woman! Let's see about cooling you off!"

Lilly's brow knit together unsure of how a Temptress would cool off when she was on the brink of physically wrestling him back into the lodge, when Jackson suddenly shifted down to one knee, twisted away to touch the ground with his hands then popped back up like a giant jack-in-the-box.

"What are you—" she began to ask but when the snowball hit her in the face the world sputtered to a stop.

Cold.

Oh!

Face.

Cold.

"Whoops! I was aiming for your shoulder," he said quickly, a man horrified and struggling not to smile. "Lilly? Are you okay?"

"You! Hit me with a snowball? A *snowball*?!" Astonishment was the only thing holding her together.

"So much for that million dollar arm. I'm so sorry, Lilly." He tipped his head to one side as he gently tried to help get the snow out of her hair. "I was hoping…I thought you'd laugh…" His words trailed off as he cautiously waited for her shock to wear off. "Lilly?"

This was not an experience she was familiar with, nor a sensation she would have anticipated. Lilly paused for fury to seize her by the throat but instead, it was mirth. *The audacity of it! The impossibility that a Demon Temptress of the First Plane would be here with snow melting down her collar and slopping over her ear and down her spine…*

Surprise was a gift and her sense of humor embraced it for the fleeting prize it offered.

Without hesitation, she turned away as if to recover or hide her tears and mirrored his maneuver, grabbing snow off the ground but she didn't trust herself to throw it. Instead she launched at him with a giggle, dumping her handfuls down the front of his parka and into his ski suit.

Jackson's yelp of protest was a delicious slice of revenge and from there, it deteriorated into playful chaos as she ran into the arena, located a small stash of unused ammo and Jackson did the same.

Snowballs flew, almost none hit their intended targets but before it was over they were both dusted with icy debris and were breathless from the battle.

A whistle blew and Lilly saw a very maternal looking Miss Laurel Marsh standing on the ladder calling an end to their game. The pair stood, guiltily, to the roar of the crowd that had instantly gathered to enjoy the show.

Jackson took it in stride, held up a hand to wave to everyone and then lifted Lilly's hand in the air. "The lady wins!"

"I'd say so!" Someone in the audience added and laughter rang out.

Lilly didn't wait for another whistle to blow before she began her retreat. Which would have been perfect except she hit a patch of icy snow and would have done a back flip if Jackson hadn't caught her elbow to steady her.

"I've got you."

"You keep saying that, Jackson Kent." Lilly straightened up, her balance restored. "But between you, me and the mountain, I'm going to have to agree. You have me. The question is, what are you going to do with me?"

He shook his head slowly, his smile so warm and genuine she thought her knees would turn to rubber. "Give me one more day, Lilly, and I'll show you."

"Mr. Kent," Laurel interrupted without a ripple of regret in her tone. "They need you at the sign up booth. The Sparks family is here and the Make-A-Wish rep wanted to talk to you before things get rolling."

"Okay." He turned back to Lilly and kissed her on the cheek. "I gotta go. Have fun, Lilly and I'll see you tonight at the dinner, yes?"

"Yes."

Lilly's hands clenched uselessly in her pockets as she watched the seamless transition where Jackson nodded and took up the mantle of the day, his responsibilities and his joyful commitment to a child who needed him.

A Temptress worth her salt would have kicked him in the shins.

But Lilly felt only awe and admiration for the man as she watched him walk away.

Oh, God.

Chapter Ten

Her nerves were getting the better of her.

She'd spent the rest of the afternoon in a bubble bath trying to meditate on nothing to clear her mind from the strange thrills of kissing Jackson Kent and the growing terror that if she didn't manage more than kisses, she was in the worst kind of trouble.

Failure is not an option.

Right?

It was her last night to achieve him and get him down.

Messages from the home office had grown more and more cryptic and Ben had abandoned all pretexts of cheerful confidence. His last voice mail had sounded more like a desperate prank call from a sobbing hysteric rather than a demonic professional.

He's afraid I've lost.

Lillith assessed her full-length reflection and met her own gaze. "I haven't lost."

Not yet anyway.

Tonight's wardrobe choice was as far from subtle as a diamond was from potting soil. The gown was a glittering column of gold, a clinging sheath of beaded silk that looked as if it had been painted onto her body. Her hair was pulled up in a loose coil that was one diamond encrusted hair comb away from tumbling down her back—and it looked it.

Everything about her dress murmured that she was one deep breath away from ruin. One kiss away from sin. One invitation away from making a man's hidden fantasies all come true.

Lilly added a trail of her perfume to the pulse points at her neck and wrists, then dipped it into the wanton cut of her cleavage. "What the hell...yes?" she smiled and then touched the glass wand to the backs of her knees and the curve of her bare thighs. "Wouldn't want to leave a trick out of the bag tonight!"

She glanced at the clock on her phone and then forced herself to count to a thousand before she picked up her matching gold evening bag and headed out of her hotel room to make her way downstairs to the final dinner of the Snow Angels Charity Weekend.

The ballroom was crowded and she noted that it was more of a mixed gathering with families from the tournament with children who participated blended in with celebrities and the wealthy weekend guests of the foundation. The local news station camera crew was once again on hand to get footage of the trophies being handed out and to capture the glamour of the attendees.

She sauntered past all of them to reach the head table where Jackson was waiting. He stood immediately, as did all the men at her arrival, and she politely demurred to take her seat as quickly as she could. "So sorry to have kept everyone waiting."

"You look...phenomenal, Lilly." Jackson cleared his throat. "I would have walked you down but the hotel said you'd blocked your calls."

She nodded. "I wanted to rest before your big night," Lilly paused to reward him with her best pout, "even if we've sworn not to make it as big a night for you as it *could* be."

Jackson shifted in his seat. "Oh, no you don't! I have to get up on stage in five minutes and hand out the medals for today's winners and then we're announcing the silent auction winners. No way are you heartless enough to torture me into a mindless, drooling troll."

"Maybe," she conceded. "But after you've done your charitable duty, I suggest you brace yourself, sir. I have evil plans for your body."

He laughed and Lillith just smiled.

The path to Hell is smooth and slippery as silk...and I'm ready to take you for a ride, dear man.

"By the way, I wanted to tell you that we experienced a bit of a miracle today," he said.

"Did we?" Lilly signaled the waiters for wine and had the pleasure of watching three of them fight to be the one to get to her first. *I'm on my game tonight!* "Miracle isn't a word I'm used to hearing."

He leaned over conspiratorially. "Our kiss on the slopes today. Can you believe not one person had a camera or phone with them? Laurel said there wasn't a single post, tweet, photo or blip on the Internet today!"

"Wow."

"Wow is right! That, my dear Miss Fields, is a bona fide miracle in my book!"

Or confirmation that the demonic magic of a suppression field isn't dampened by cold weather and yours truly getting a snowball in her hair.

She lifted her wine glass in a toast. "Here's to miracles. Maybe we can fit in another one before the clock strikes midnight?"

He held his glass up to touch hers, his eyes gleaming with desire. "That's a distinct possibility even though I swore I wouldn't push my luck."

Lilly smiled and took a drink from the toast to savor the connection between them. "You are a very fortunate and blessed man, Jackson. As for luck—you're the one who asked me not to flirt too much so I hope you take note that I left off about a dozen great lines about you getting lucky tonight. I want extra credit for taking the high road, Jackson." She touched her lower lip with her tongue, the trick of a courtesan perfected into a sexual weapon. "Yes?"

He nodded, a man stunned and uncomplaining. "Yes. High road. I'm...grateful you're taking it easy on me."

"You have no idea."

True to his word, he had to leave the table and head for the stage. Lilly sipped her wine and leaned back in her chair to enjoy the show. The medal presentations went quickly and every child who won elicited a new round of sighs and exclamations as they went up so smartly in their evening best with their innocent faces looking out on the crowd. Even Lilly struggled not to fall prey to their darling reactions to winning "Best Bubble Dragon Slayer" or "Best Snow Jumper" or "Biggest Snowman".

It's ridiculous. Let's remember it's all about the last minute flurry of check-writing that's going on this very second...and nothing more!

Except when a little girl in a wheelchair was called forward for "Sweetest Snow Princess" and Lilly had to bite the inside of her cheek to keep her eyes from filling with tears. Jackson put a crown of glittering rhinestone snowflakes on her tiny head and the room held its breath as he kissed her cheek.

"Marry me!" the little girl squeaked out loud enough for his microphone to pick it up.

Laughter and applause rang out and the television crews exchanged grins at the personal interest and sports gold they'd just struck.

Jackson knelt next to her, his expression one of genuine affection. "I am very flattered, Princess Riley, but my heart is already spoken for and I'd be in Big Trouble if she caught me flirting up here."

"Okay. I'm gonna marry Ward Keller then. He has comic books."

"Okay." Jackson nodded, graciously accepting the news of his replacement. "It's hard to beat comic books."

He stood and the applause in the room thundered as Riley was pushed back to her seat. Jackson blushed as he returned to the podium. "Well, I'm not sure how to top that act, but I have to thank everyone who bid in the silent auction and while we would normally just let you check the board over there later to see if you won, I just have to single out one of our winners tonight because that kind of generosity—I didn't see it coming and not for the piece of art I tucked in as a joke. This man has humbled me by showing he's more than a pretty face," Jackson said. "I underestimated him and I hope he'll forgive me. Stefan Walker! Come up here and let me shake your hand, guy!"

An uproar of cheering and the energy jolted through the room as everyone craned their necks to get a glimpse of the celebrity winner. It was more thrilling for Lilly. Stefan Walker's face was locked in an expression of complete shock and he was saved only by the way his seatmates kept pounding him on the back in congratulations. He shook his head and would have tried to keep his seat, but it was interpreted as intense humility so his seatmates began to physically shove him out of his chair and up onto the stage.

Stefan Walker stumbled up the stairs and gave the perfect impression of a man who just couldn't believe he was the happy winner of the world's ugliest finger painting.

Lilly clapped along with her table but her smile was a wicked thing.

Because she knew that for once in his life, Stefan Walker wasn't acting.

The television crews instantly sprang into action and the glow of the lights bathed a secretly unhappy film star's clumsy approach to the podium to shake Jackson's hand.

"Mr. Walker, thank you so much!"

"Don't mention it?" Stefan joked. "I…um…would it hurt your feelings if I admit I was hoping someone would outbid me so that I didn't have to hang that thing in my house?"

Jackson laughed and put an arm around Stefan in a show of camaraderie and the room exploded in flash bulbs. "You have my permission to hang it in your basement if you want to! For what you paid, you get to use it as the world's most expensive car floor mat, guy!"

"Sure." Stefan's loss of eloquence was hilarious as no one really noticed.

"Well, I'll see you at the Super Bowl next year as a consolation prize. If not on the field, then in a box, Walker!"

"I hate football," Stefan whispered but the mic picked it up. Laughter sprang up everywhere and even Jackson thought the man was kidding, solidifying Stefan Walker's amazing redemption as a generous and compassionate human being.

"Come for the half-time show then!" Jackson countered cheerfully and then into the podium's mic, "Stefan Walker, ladies and gentlemen! A real star!"

Stefan's face lost some color but he couldn't ask exactly what that amount was, couldn't risk looking like an ass if he admitted that he hadn't bid so much as a penny and that there'd been a mistake. He couldn't argue that he suspected it was all a prank or even complain without looking like a world class jerk.

"Well, thank you everyone! The dancing starts now, enjoy yourselves for the rest of the night and I hope to see all of our Snow Angel Foundation guests tomorrow at the farewell brunch!" Jackson wrapped it up quickly and escorted Stefan off the stage where several people had gathered to shake his hand and offer their thanks to the movie star for his contribution.

Stefan's gaze landed on Lillith beyond the fray, sitting like a cool and casual queen watching him with a knowing smile on her lips and he made quick work of the autographs and chaos to excuse himself and walk over to the table.

"May I have this dance, Miss Fields?" he asked.

Lilly studied him for a moment. *Unstable idiot but he's unlikely to get physical with a camera crew in the room. Vanity has its uses. And one dance may kill more than a few birds if it goes well. Magic off, gentleman. I'm going in!*

"Why not?" she replied as graciously as she could, rising from her seat. She smiled at Jackson to ensure that there was no misunderstanding and waited until he smiled back before she took Stefan's hand and allowed him to lead her out onto the parquet floor.

He was a lovely dancer and Lilly sighed. *It's a shame he won't be able to wait past the fourth bar of music before his temper gets the better of—*

"Why am I the owner of dung on canvas, Miss Fields? Any ideas?" he hissed in her ear.

"Because you wanted to prove that you aren't a total waste of human flesh and bone?" she asked innocently. "No? Was there another motivation?"

"I know it was you."

"Pardon? It was me what?" Lilly replied, politely keeping at least eighteen inches of space between them. "What are you saying? Are you saying that you didn't even *bid* on that painting?"

"Keep your voice down!" he snarled, then smiled so that anyone looking on would mistake it all for friendly dance floor conversation. "Mind telling me what I paid for that thing?"

"Oh, relax! Nothing crushing. Don't be a big baby!"

Stefan's expression darkened. "He brought me up on stage and is looking at me like a saint. How. Much. Money."

"You have a handsome salary for your film work, a fat bank balance to finance two lifetimes, three mansions, a share in an island resort, a private jet, a luxury yacht and more cars than you can remember in that obscene air-conditioned garage of yours. You are a wealthy man, Walker. Take a deep breath." She glanced over his shoulder to ensure that Jackson was near and had his eyes on her. She whispered an amount that only Stefan could hear and waited for the impact because it was the exact number down to the penny of an offshore account he'd been illegally hoarding tax-free, hiding it from his own accountants and lawyers for some imaginary 'rainy day'.

Whoops! Look at that! I made it rain!

"What?" Stefan stopped dancing. He stopped in his tracks which naturally meant everyone on the dance floor became an awkward participant in the moment. "What did you say? That's impossible! You couldn't know that number! You, bitch! I'm not paying that! It's not a legal contract and I'll prove it wasn't my handwriting on some lame sign up sheet! I'm not paying one shitty penny to this ridiculous foundation dreamt up by an ape! Who cares about a bunch of genetically defective mutts? Cancer is God's way of thinning out the herd and I am *not* stupid enough to get in the Big Guy's path and piss my fortune down a hole!"

Lilly took a single step back just as Jackson Kent and several other men surged forward to defend her. "That was way too easy," she said calmly, her pronouncement lost in the noise and shouting.

"What did you just say, Walker?" Jackson's voice was cold as steel. "The ape wants to hear you say that one more time."

"I—didn't mean…" Stefan looked up to see not only the wall of looks aimed at him ranging from fury to disgust and horror, but Jackson directly in front of him. Beyond it all, the cameraman lifted his camera alongside the soundman's boom mic to make sure that when it hit the evening news, every glorious detail would be recorded for posterity's sake. "I was just angry! Someone played a prank on us both, Kent! I never bid… She…"

He faltered, his brain finally catching up. He'd already said unforgiveable things. But if he pointed the finger at Lilly, everything really unraveled. He would have to explain why she would do such a thing and why she had a recording of him on her phone that might be construed to support her claims. If criminal charges were pressed, several women he'd bullied in the past might raise their hands and start talking to the press. Even if he left that slice of bad off the table, he would still have to come up with a reason why such an odd dollar amount on a bid card would trigger his reaction, which might lead to questions about why he was hiding money in the first place and why he hadn't reported it to the government and why—why his A-List life had probably just come to a screeching end.

Lilly watched him weighing it out and she could practically read his mind. *How many scandals does it take to ruin a man? He's already crucified by the racist slur and that rant about those sick children alone, and now he's scrambling to see if he can keep the I.R.S. from issuing a warrant, if every woman he's ever assaulted won't start lining up to get her pound of flesh and if he'll still have a career on Monday.*

"I'll pay it!" Stefan announced loudly with a broad smile. "Of course, I'll honor my commitment to those precious—"

"Get out. I don't want a single shitty penny of your money for my Snow Angels, Mr. Walker," Jackson cut him off calmly. "Gentlemen, please escort Mr. Walker out of the party and let the hotel know that he'll be checking out tonight."

It was two more minutes of video gold for the cameras as the sexiest man in the world transformed into a thug being hauled out of party for showing more of his ass than anyone had dreamt of seeing. The music had never stopped playing and the irony of the

DJ's choice to spin "Make It Rain" by Ed Sheeran as Stefan Walker pushed away from his escorts and did his best to storm out like a wronged debutante was too fabulous.

Jackson made every effort to personally speak to everyone on the dance floor, privately apologizing for the incident and reassuring them that Stefan Walker's bad behavior was not going to spoil the good work they had all done. He refused to speak to the press, but quickly approached every child who was still present at the party to give them a hug and ensure that none of Stefan's remarks had hit their mark and were not relayed to their vulnerable ears.

Instead of fracturing the event's participants, the scene galvanized them and they circled around each other with hugs, comforting words and smiles.

Jackson had in effect, circled the wagons.

Lilly kept her distance, awash in a tangle of pride and guilt.

He's magnificent in action and—he's apologizing for another man's faults, soothing feelings and letting some of them vent their surprise and fury. A wicked man would be calling his lawyer to make sure his liability and exposure was limited by Walker's actions or he'd be blustering speeches to distance himself from the hateful bigot. But what does my Jackson do? He hugs people and makes sure everyone is okay.

Lilly froze.

He wasn't her Jackson. *Did I just do that? Did I just compose the words 'my Jackson' in my head? What kind of demon would do that?!*

"Lilly? Are you okay?" Jackson was at her elbow. "I'm sorry about everything. I'd have just grabbed you and run out of the room if—that was so ugly and I needed to make sure all my parents and their children were set. I just didn't want people to think…the worst."

"The worst?"

"You know. That we'd forged his bid to force him into giving the Foundation money or that anything he said wasn't a total surprise. My God! I never really liked him but that was—is there another word for ugly because I just can't think right now?"

"No one thinks the worst of you, the Snow Angels Foundation, or the hospital. There are approximately one hundred and forty-eight ways to convey 'ugly' but, Jackson," Lillith reached up to touch his face with her fingertips, "those aren't the words that come to mind when I look at you."

Jackson lifted her hand to turn it over, kissing her palm. "What a night!"

"It's just starting although the news teams are running out the door to get to their vans to upload the drama, so I'd say we have our Miracle Part Two." Lilly pointed out the retreat of the press. "Now, we can kiss like teenagers in the middle of this room and never make the evening news."

He laughed and she was glad to hear it. "Let's just dance."

"Okay," she said with a sly smile. "A safe choice but I'll take it."

It was a wonderful slow song and Jackson pulled her into his arms. He didn't have any of the movie star's dance skills, but Lilly could not care less. The high-school-prom-shuffle-sway was dreamy when you were in Jackson Kent's arms. Lilly sighed and put her cheek against his shoulder.

"We're just one mirror-ball away from perfection, don't you think?"

"I don't need another thing. I'm there," he said softly.

"Don't say that until I have my wicked way with you after this dance," she teased him, sliding her palms across his back.

"Lilly. Behave."

Lilly lifted her head, a flash of irritation spoiling the game. "No."

"Sweetie, Monday, remember?"

"Jackson! Miracle, remember? No press. It's just us. Well, us and a few hundred people who all think you walk on water but I'm sure they wouldn't begrudge their favorite hero a delicious minor slip with the damsel he rescued from that sludge-mouthed dragon." She tipped her head back to really look up into his eyes. "You need a sports analogy? The other team dropped the ball. The goal line is defenseless and nothing is going to stop you from scoring. There! How did that sound?"

Jackson shook his head and gently led her off of the dance floor. "I don't walk on water but if anyone thinks that, then I'm in big trouble."

Sexual frustration hit her like a tidal wave. *Not again. I cannot believe he's about to sweetly put me off again.*

"Jackson. My bad. I should not have invoked that—image. But I can't lie, I am really hoping you'll pretend that it's Sunday night and if you want, we can wait until midnight but—this. This is my Hail Mary."

"What's going on, Lilly? The chemistry between us is…I don't even know how to describe it. You don't need to worry about rushing, babe and you of all people, don't need to worry about some last, desperation play for me. You have me, Lillith."

"Take me upstairs, Jackson."

"Lilly…"

"I'm betting there was going to be more behind my name, Jackson." She waited patiently, using the awkward silence to really look at him. He was handsome. It was a given that he would expect to be admired but the expression in his gaze was nothing she expected.

He wasn't preening. He wanted her but there was nothing smug or assured beyond the heat she read there. He could have her easily but he held himself in check. Masculine power emanated from him, raw and beautiful, but Jackson Kent mesmerized her because he ignored that power and commanded her attention with his humanity.

I am a Seductress.

I hold the reins.

Except she didn't.

"Every time I look at you, Lilly, all bets are off."

A spiral of delicious heat unwound inside of her, at once familiar and alien. Lust was her specialty but this…was different. She did not have the whip hand over this sensation. Instead it was Lilly who burned for him.

Touch me.

"What does that mean?"

He shook his head slowly and led her gently back to their chairs at the table to sit back down. "I don't want to play games here. I want to win more than one chance or one night with you, Lilly. You make me feel as if everything hangs in the balance."

"And that scares you." It wasn't a question.

He smiled. "It should but it doesn't. I think the thing I feel most is relief."

"Relief?" Lilly's back straightened as if someone had shot a gun behind her. "Where the hell does *relief* come into this?" If the man had announced he was a lemur she couldn't be more shocked. *Damn it! I'm dishing out my best stuff over here! The only one feeling relief should be me when he slides his hotel room key across this table and I take him upstairs for a little ride.*

"I'd almost given up waiting for it, Lilly. For this. For this magical, amazing connection that everyone always sighs about—in songs, in wedding toasts, in sappy books, you name it. I'm a man and I was pretty content to substitute fun or sex or affection or…whatever seemed workable in the moment. I told myself it was 'love' and that everyone else was just overcompensating or deluding themselves into clinging to fairy tales. When a woman said she wanted more, I easily let go and congratulated myself on being the only practical man left standing." Jackson sighed. "I wasn't heartless but I was starting to worry that I might not have a talent for relationships. I thought maybe I'd been blessed and lucky in so many things that I'd have to be an ungrateful jerk to complain if I hadn't been as lucky in love."

"You don't have to be an ungrateful jerk to complain. People complain all the time, Jackson. Some people get paid to complain. Remember Andy Rooney?" Lilly was rambling and she knew it. She was off course and lost unless he was just bringing up love as a preamble to asking her to take her clothes off. "That man complained about the color of the sky, that socks came in pairs and once dedicated an entire segment to thumbtacks and paperclips and how he had too many of them."

"Lilly?" Jackson caught one of her hands in his. "I don't have too many paperclips."

"No?" Lilly bit her lower lip. "Are you sure? What about a fetish involving scotch tape? A secret collection of blow up dolls? An obsession with mermaids? The ability to see dead people?"

Jackson laughed. "Would any of that help?"

"Yes! Because then you would *not* be perfect and I would—know what I'm dealing with here!" Lilly blurted it out. "I need to know what I'm dealing with, Jackson."

Jackson shook his head. "Just an ordinary guy over here, Lilly."

"In what way, Jackson Kent, are you 'ordinary'?"

"You mean besides putting my pants on one leg at a time and all of that?"

A jolt of irrational need struck her at the very mention of Jackson without his pants on and Lilly wanted to scream in frustration. "I don't believe that you put your pants on one leg at a time. Perhaps I'll need a demonstration."

"That's a demo I'm happy to provide, Lilly. But come on. You are winding me up over there and I—I need an answer."

"An answer?" Lilly blinked.

"If it's no, it's no. I'm not made of glass but I can take it."

"I missed the question."

"Do you feel the same way, Lilly?"

The air in the room diminished and every rational thought she tried to wrangle eluded her grasp. "The same way as what?" she asked him softly.

"I think this might be love, Lilly. It's fast and crazy and everything I used to mock but I swear if you said that I only needed to stand on this table and sing "Somewhere Over the Rainbow", I'd do it and never look back."

"Th-that would go viral online. Don't do that!" Lilly squeezed his fingers protectively, fighting a giddy reaction that had nothing to do with seductions. "Y-you. Love. *Me*?!" Lilly caught her breath. "I…never…thought it…possible."

"Being loved?" he pressed.

"It really isn't possible. People get confused. I am *not* lovable." Lilly's hands were ice cold and she sensed an abyss of doom at her back. If she didn't recover the mission immediately and gain her footing, she may not survive. "You could be saying that because you are a nice person and you think you have to make a declaration in order to get me on my back. I'm flattered. But let's get you upstairs where you can demonstrate your pant removal skills in private and leave the Q&A for afterward."

He didn't move a single muscle to indicate compliance. "Tell me how you feel about me, Lilly."

Her mouth dropped open briefly and terror joined the mix of confusing emotions churning inside of her. *Demons lie like rugs. Come on, Lillith. Tell him you adore him and you're ready to prove your undying love by taking him to the moon and back. Let's roll!*

Except nothing rolled.

"You know how some women have…baggage?" she asked in a whisper.

He nodded solemnly.

"They're damaged somehow? Nothing but trouble and heartache? And any man with twelve points of IQ should run when he sees them coming?"

"Yup."

"I'm that." Lilly exhaled slowly. "I'm that in spades. I have boatloads of ridiculously solid reasons why my feelings are irrelevant in this scenario. I mean it. Zero importance on…the impossible question of why we are even wasting time thinking about me when you… " Lilly accepted that she'd stopped making sense and took another deep breath to try a different tactic. "Let's just pop upstairs and ignore my feelings together, shall we? I can think of nine distracting activities we can try and that was without any effort, Jackson. If inspired, I'm fairly certain we can forget how to spell our own names if I apply myself to the task. What do you say?"

He didn't move.

Lilly closed her eyes for a brief moment, trying to understand when she'd stepped off the cliff. *Was it the revolving door? Was it the auction? Which smile? The first kiss? The second, or third or sixth kiss? The snowball fight? When did I lose my heart to this man? And now, what? How to measure what the cost will be—for either one of us!*

Lilly opened her eyes and looked at him, hating the tears in her eyes, hating the strange broken hitch in her chest and the sweetness in his face. "Oh, to Hell with it! I love you. I love you! I—" she clapped a hand over her mouth refusing to allow the hysterical babbling to continue. Lilly pulled away from the table and stood, less gracefully than she'd have wished but without tipping the table over and spilling their drinks so that was a small victory. "Thanks for the snowball fight."

She turned and left, her sole aim toward getting out of his line of sight so that she could transport to her room, report to the office for damage control and see if Asmodeus was screaming for her head on a platter. *Dead Demon Walking here, folks!*

But she never eluded him. Jackson was up like a shot and on her heels, catching her in the lobby. He'd won her and lost her in one move and Jackson was not a man who liked to lose and certainly not when it came to this woman, he wasn't going to surrender without a single fight.

He gently reached out to snag her upper arm and turn her back toward him. "Lillith! I'm not sure why you telling me you love me now means we're playing tag—but I am happy to chase you to the ends of the earth if that's what it takes."

"Apparently you weren't listening to the part about the baggage and the emergency evacuation order." Lilly did her best to dig in her heels. "Man your lifeboats."

"Lilly, you might be a thousand things but you are not a sinking ship."

"I'm going to need a few minutes. I need to…take this in." Lilly meant to pull away from him but found herself sighing into his touch. "I can't talk to you here."

"Let's go upstairs."

Chapter Eleven

Her eyes widened. "W-what?"

"Let's go upstairs. Not for the pants demo, Lilly. Let's go upstairs to my room so that we can talk in private."

She nodded slowly and he led the way to the bank of elevators aware that he was probably on shaky ground. He'd vowed to be a gentleman and keep his pants on but Jackson knew that just one or two of Lilly's kisses could probably unravel that plan.

In the elevator, she was so quiet and still that it was all he could do just to hold her against him. He wanted to feel joy. He'd thrown caution to the winds and told her he loved her and she'd done the same. Albeit, she'd admitted she loved him after a very weird scuffle about baggage and a nearly irresistible offer to sleep with him; but Jackson wasn't going to throw the baby out with the bath water.

They made it to his suite and the door was latched and locked behind them when she finally broke her silence.

"The worst part isn't that I can tell when someone is lying," Lilly said as she raked her fingers through her hair.

"I would never lie to you, Lilly."

The statement had the opposite effect he was braced for. Her eyes filled with tears that now spilled unchecked onto her cheeks.

"See? That was also not a lie! You would never lie! What kind of man says that sort of thing and isn't lying when he says it?!" Lilly hiccupped and then froze, one hand clapped over her lips in shock and horror.

Jackson smiled. "I'm pretty sure the world is full of men who don't lie."

"I'm pretty sure you're wrong but let's agree to disagree." Her argument failed to convey any gravitas as she hiccupped again, a miserable squeak that only made her more endearing in his eyes.

His Lilly did *not* like to be vulnerable and let him see her human frailties.

"Okay, Lilly. I'll bite. What is the worst part? I mean, besides having an uncanny ability to know that I honestly love you?"

"The worst part…is that I wasn't lying when I said I loved you back," she whispered.

"That's the worst part?" he asked. "Seriously?"

"You have no idea."

"Water."

"What?" Lilly asked before another squeak got past her lips.

"I need to get you a glass of water, woman. I have a whole fantasy brewing of how this scene is going to play out and you looking like a tortured victim after every hiccup is not part of the picture." Jackson strode over to the wet bar against the wall and began to fill an old-fashioned with ice and water. "Let's take care of you and then we can figure out how to get you to say you love me at least six thousand more times and to smile when you say it."

Lilly crossed her arms stubbornly. "Oh, joy. I've fallen for a card carrying member of the Love Police."

Squeak.

He walked back to her and handed her the glass. "Drink."

She dutifully obeyed then handed the glass back when she had her breathing under control. "You are very bossy, Kent."

"Only when I have to be, Fields." Jackson set the glass down on a coffee table and then stepped up to her, close enough to pull her into his arms—but wary of pressuring her. "Look, I don't know what baggage you're carrying, or what damage you're hiding, but I've fallen in love with you Lilly Fields. That means all of you and at this point, you just need to tell me what obstacles I need to overcome and I'll make it happen. I want to prove to you that love is more than words because I've waited too long for this. I finally feel it Lilly, and I don't want it to end. So let's have it."

"I think I'm still in shock."

"Come on, Lilly. What's on deck? Abusive boyfriends? An ex-husband? You have a criminal record? A drug problem? Where are we at?"

Her mouth fell open and her eyes sparked in a spirited show of temper. "*We* are at a very strange crossroads between 'You Have Got to Be Kidding Me' Street and 'I Don't Think You Are Ready For This' Boulevard."

The sound of her phone vibrating made her gasp and before he could urge her to ignore it, she retrieved it from her pocket to check the screen.

"Lilly. Whatever it is, it can wait," Jackson said.

The color drained from her cheeks but she shut the phone off and put it away. "I have five minutes."

"Five minutes? You have…somewhere to be at this hour?"

She shook her head. "Jackson. This is it. Tell me. Is there some terrible dark secret you're hiding from the world? Some horrible crime? Some twisted need or repulsive fetish that would end you if the public uncovered it?"

"The public!? No! What sort of questions are those? And what would the public have to do with anything that… Lilly, what are you asking me?"

"I don't know! I'm drawing a blank over here! I think I'm asking if you like to make snuff films in your spare time! I'm asking if you…are anything other than what you appear to be!"

"No! I'm—me! What you see is what you get, Lilly. I'm not perfect but—"

"But you are! It's ridiculous but you are!"

"That's not true! No one's perfect but I'm getting a little irritated that you keep wanting me to confess to eating live kittens on Christmas mornings."

"Do you?" Lilly suddenly looked so hopeful, he nearly laughed.

Nearly.

"Lillith! What the hell!?"

Her head dropped, a woman defeated. "Hell."

He pulled her against his chest and tipped her chin up until she was looking up into his eyes. "I never thought I'd disappoint a woman by somehow failing to eat kittens so you'll have to clue me in, Lilly. What's going on here?"

She smiled. "I need you to remember that I wasn't lying when I said I loved you. I need you to know that it's never happened to me before. *Never.*"

"Like the hiccups?"

"Exactly like the hiccups. From the start, you've affected me like no other man and I will cherish that for every minute that is left to me." Lilly reached up to cradle his face in her hands. "And I'm going to remember the way you're looking at me now because in ten seconds, you'll never do it again. Not like that anyway."

"How am I going to look at you?" Jackson braced himself. Here it came. A confession about how she was just a tabloid reporter or a high-paid call girl or… He just didn't care. Whatever Lilly had been before she'd come into his life was smoke and mirrors. People changed and reformed and recovered and—

"Jackson, when your mother warned you about bad girls, whatever she said, I'm a thousand times worse. I'm the Ultimate Bad Girl."

Jackson smiled. "When you say that, it sounds like I just won the lottery, Lilly."

Lilly sighed. "Okay. Direct speech then." Lilly squeezed his upper arms as if to keep herself from falling. "Here goes everything. I am not a human being. Jackson, I am a demon."

His brain didn't even repeat what she'd said. For the first time in his life, he experienced dead air and a mental white noise that shut out language.

"Say that again?" he tried.

"I'm a demon." Lillith's grip held them in place without much force. "I'm a card carrying employee of a company that you probably know as Hell. Not that the décor is anything you'd imagine but that's Upper Management's call, Jackson."

"What corporation? Demons have cards?" Jackson blinked twice. "They carry…wallets? Demons carry wallets?"

Lilly smiled. "Only on field trips."

"Are you seeing a doctor, Lilly? Are you on medication?"

"I'm a Temptress, Jackson. I'm a Take-Down Agent in the Temptations Department of Hades Enterprises, LLc and for the record, you're the first mortal to get that little tidbit." Lilly released him and stepped back. "Take-Downs are complicated missions and one of the rare moments that the Corporation interferes with the natural course of events. They don't do it lightly and failure isn't an option. I seduce evil men and see to their downfall when Upper Management makes the call. When someone gets flagged for a Take-Down, it's Hell's chance to make a positive contribution—albeit not in ways most people would brag about."

"I'm not evil. I'm not perfect but I'm not evil, so I think we're off base here, Lilly."

"Good point." She nodded. "Clearly, the incomplete file I was given by my supervisor should have been my first clue."

"Lilly, I keep hoping—is it wrong that I keep hoping for a confetti cannon to go off and for you to bring out the hidden camera crew?"

She rolled her eyes. "Thank you for that. A Temptress should always keep a good sense of humor in her arsenal. Not that demons really lack for an appreciation of comedy. It's just that we're not usually the punchline."

"I know you're speaking English but why is none of this making any sense?" Jackson pressed his fingers against his temples. "Is there a remedial pamphlet you can give me because I think I heard something about temptations and Hades but I can't be sure because after the word 'demon', I might have suffered from a stroke."

"You didn't have a stroke."

"How do you know?" Jackson looked at her, waiting for the punchline then praying for a punchline. "Then again, I don't smell oranges. I think I read once that if you smell oranges out of the blue, or burnt toast, you should call 9-1-1."

"Good idea. You call 9-1-1. Tell them a crazy woman forced her way into your room and…claimed to be possessed or something! Get a crowd of people around you for the next few hours. Call Laurel. She'll organize a command center and back up every theory you have about me. She's very clever, Jackson. Stay safe." She closed the gap between them and moved to kiss him on the cheek as her tears began to fall again. "Good bye."

The smart thing to do was to let Crazy Woman go without a fight.

But even with the madness clinging to her like perfume, his heart wasn't having it. He kissed her again, wanting to claim her, to keep her to prove that he wasn't alone in any of it. His desire for her was off the charts but there was so much more going on and Jackson refused to relinquish any part of her until he could say what emotion it was that had him by the throat.

"Lilly, this is crazy. Actually, let's take the word crazy off the table."

"As in we just assume that both of us are completely sane?"

"Yes. So that makes you warm and beautiful, kind and sweet, you are a lot of things but human is obviously one of them and even if we made the leap to secret agent of the Underworld, I'd like to slow down and figure out why you look so terrified. Stay, Lilly. Let's—talk this out! If it's metaphors and your way of trying to let me down gently, then we'll laugh it off and order in a late night dinner and—"

She gently pressed a single finger against his lips. "Jackson, that kiss was worth it all. Thank you."

She headed toward the door and he called out, "Lilly! Where are you going?"

She looked back over her shoulder, jaunty and confident, her power and beauty so potent, he had to catch his breath. "I have Hell to pay." She blew him a kiss and was gone, the door firmly closing behind her.

The sound of the door's latch vaulted him into motion. He threw the door open to stop her and Jackson cried out in shock as he was faced with an empty hall, a deserted corridor and no sign of Lilly Fields.

Jackson froze, immediately aware that not only was there no one in the hallway, but the elevators weren't illuminated to betray that they'd been summoned. But the door to the stairs was a good forty yards and in two seconds—it was too vast a distance for Lilly to have covered.

Not at an Olympian sprint.

Not in those high heels she was wearing.

So where did she go?

The phone in his room started ringing and Jackson Kent felt like a man with his toes on the edge of a cliff. Reality was at his back and in an empty hall where women vanished into thin air was demons, madness and a very unappealing possibility that nothing in the world he knew was going to hold water.

In slow motion, he closed the door and leaned his forehead against the unyielding wood. The phone's ringing was an unrelenting petition for his attention and Jackson walked back into the room to take the call, not out of a desire to talk to anyone but more out of the shock that the woman of his dreams had just faded into a nightmare.

Or I really am crazy...and nothing will ever make sense again.

Lilly reappeared in her hotel room, took one deep breath before her phone rang. The caller ID was an ancient symbol and Lillith answered it instantly. "Good evening, Dread Lord. Is there a problem with my expense report?"

"Do not dare to get cheeky with me, Temptress." Asmodeus was apparently not in the mood for light banter.

Then again, when was he ever in the mood for light banter?

Lilly nearly dropped the phone in shock at her own brazen lack of fear. "Apologies."

"What are you doing, Temptress? Why isn't he down?"

She closed her eyes. "The event ends tomorrow. I was taking my time."

"You are out of time. Word has reached us that you have failed. There are rumors of worse but you will stand before me when we discuss the matter at hand."

"I have not yet failed. The event officially finishes tomorrow and I am confident that I can surprise you all with just a few more hours at my disposal." Her grip on the phone tightened until her knuckles looked white. "I formally petition for more time. If you pull me now, then the failure is yours not mine."

Silence answered her but Lilly waited. She opened her eyes and caught her own reflection in the mirror. She looked calm and unbroken. The irony made the tears start and her terror leapt up a fire fed by the wicked fuel of her newfound weakness.

"The event officially ends tomorrow morning at ten. I will *personally* come to collect you at one minute after ten, Lillith."

"As you wish, Dread Lord. Wear something warm." She disconnected the phone before her knees gave out and she collapsed to the floor.

Oh, this was an epic failure they'll talk about for millenniums but that last one liner—that might just outlive Asmodeus...

Chapter Twelve

"Mr. Kent. Earth to Jackson Kent." Laurel gently shoved her elbow into his side. "People are starting to notice that you're sitting there looking like your dog just died."

"I'm…good."

"Oh, yes. I can tell. I mean that was the third donor in a row who has tried to personally thank you for a great weekend who got a response that made it seem like you were auditioning for zombie extra in Stefan's next film." She smiled at the gathering as she spoke to make sure that anyone looking over at their host wouldn't see him getting an earful from his admin. "If your dog died, just let me know and I'll announce it and we'll get a last round of sympathy donations but otherwise, I highly recommend you cut it out."

Jackson straightened in his chair and shot her a disapproving look. "You're fired."

Laurel smiled. "Ah, you're awake! Naturally since I have only thirty minutes left before the event's finished, I'm happy to leave all the clean-up and administrative headaches to you. Good timing."

"You're re-hired."

"Was that a glimmer of humor I detected? Did you almost smile, Mr. Kent?"

"No," he said stubbornly but accepted that Miss Marsh had a valid point to make. Sabotaging all the hard work of so many people just because he was in the middle of a romantic catastrophe was beyond idiotic. It was time to put on his best game face and fake his way through one last speech and make an exit. "But I'm not going to make it for half an hour so let's just wrap this up."

"What?"

He stood up to make his purpose clear and headed for the small podium in the corner that was prepared for final farewells. "Good morning, friends! I know you're all ready to run but I promise this is the last time they'll give me a microphone."

He forced himself to smile and thought of Max and the children. He would think of them for the next few minutes and nothing else. "No lie. I'm feeling a little too emotional to talk this morning. So don't be surprised when you get thank you letters in your mailboxes to compensate for the inadequate words I'm going to choke out. Thank you. For coming out this weekend, for traveling so far, for giving so much and for your faith in a community of people that no one else was investing in. That rundown hospital is now a beacon of hope, a certified critical care center and a place where families come to heal. The ripples of what we do aren't always seen right away but I can assure you, they are felt by every child and every parent who walks through the doors of Snows Metro Community Hospital. It's…we won't let them down…"

The applause started and he just bowed his head.

There goes that. No slick speech about hearts and souls and begging them to just be generous without the bribe of all this show, without the balls and the dinners and the art… Damn it. I'm just gutted.

The applause thundered as if they'd mistaken his posture for something more. He didn't bother to correct them. Let them think he was just moved by it all, or praying, or whatever. None of it felt real or meaningful.

He walked out without another word with the applause still cresting, determined to leave with what little of his dignity he could muster.

Laurel caught up with him waiting outside the elevator doors. "Mr. Kent!"

"Good job, Laurel. Let's…you handle the last bit. I'll be…"

"Jackson. Did you have a falling out with Miss Fields?"

He whipped around, ready to make a firm denial but faltered. "That obvious?"

"She's not at this breakfast and—a person would have to be blind to miss the sparks flying at the Fire Ball and then yesterday. You were all smiles and jigging around like a kid at a carnival but," Laurel paused to eye him closely. "A man coming back from a funeral has more bounce in his step."

"Lilly is—it's apparently complicated." He raked his fingers through his hair in frustration. "I'm not up for sharing."

Laurel sighed and crossed her arms, pressing her ever present tablet to her bosom. "She hasn't checked out yet. You should call her."

He shook his head. "I've called. A lot. Last night and then again this morning. No answer. I think we're past the phone call window of opportunity."

And only this morning did it occur to me that I didn't bother to get Lilly's cell number…so once she checks out, I'd say that window is pretty much nailed shut.

The elevator chimed its arrival and he shifted his stance. "Laurel, I'll meet you this afternoon to go over everything before I catch my flight home."

"Do you think Joe DiMaggio wishes he'd fought a little harder for his Marilyn?"

"What?" The elevator doors began to open and other guests stepped off.

Laurel went on, undaunted. "I mean, I'm sure she was a handful but I don't ever remember him smiling the way he did when he was with Marilyn Monroe. What do you think?"

"I think he was a dumb jock who landed a goddess and then…was stupid enough to let her go." Jackson bit the words out, hating the bitter taste of them and completely aware of who he meant. "Damn it, I have to go!"

He passed through the doors just as they began to close and saw the satisfied look on Laurel's face.

Chapter Thirteen

The elevator ride went quickly and he made no effort to compose a speech. He was in front of her hotel room door and pounding on it long before his brain could come up with the usual pro's and con's that came with trying to convince her not to return to whatever mental institution she was living at and to stay with him forever.

"Lilly!" he shouted. "Lilly, it's Jackson. I need to talk to you. I need to see you! Baby, I don't care if you have horns and a forked tail! Let's just talk about this!"

The sound of the door's security latch being lifted startled him. He'd expected to spend several minutes making his case so the easy victory threw him off a bit. But the sight of Lillith Fields in caramel fawn colored cashmere and a long black mink coat soothed his soul. She was dressed to the nines, a woman ready to travel and without a hair out of place as if she'd stepped off the pages of a magazine.

This is not what crazy looks like. Crazy wears tin foil hats, diapers and stilettos. Please, God.

"It's traditionally a forked tongue and a barbed tail and you are describing the medieval depiction of the devil, not a demon, Jackson."

"Okay." He lifted his hands in surrender. "Can I come in, Lilly? You can diagram out all the differences between the two and I'll even take notes if you want."

She rolled her eyes but stepped back to allow him entry. "I shouldn't be doing this. There…isn't much time. You can stay for just a few minutes."

Her luggage was neatly stacked in front of the closet and Jackson noted that if he'd waited, he really would have missed her completely. "I'll take whatever time you give me, Lilly."

"I'm serious, Jackson. You have to leave by ten. Promise."

Jackson glanced at the clock. He had eighteen minutes.

"Do you have a plane to catch?" he asked.

Lilly crossed her arms defiantly. "It feels ridiculously good to see you again but I do not want to talk about the time."

"What do you want to talk about?"

"Jackson Kent! You're the one pounding on my door about needing to talk!"

"I know. I just…there you are and now all I can think to say is that I blew it last night. You were testing me somehow and I—I fumbled the ball." Jackson reached for her, seeking to touch her beyond the barrier of an extremely beautiful and politically incorrect fur coat. "I want to try again, Lilly."

"No sports metaphors allowed, Kent. The game is a complete mystery to me and I don't want to waste our last precious seconds together learning how many points you get when you make a basket."

He opened his mouth and then closed it quickly. She was right about one thing only. He didn't want to waste time on the difference between a goal and a basket. But she was wrong about more than sports vocabulary. "Not our last seconds, Lilly. I love you. That hasn't changed so I don't see why we can't work through whatever this is. I'm not a quitter."

She gasped. "There is no trying again. There shouldn't have been a first try. I'm not supposed to get the hiccups, or cry, or fall in love. I'm not a challenge, Jackson. I am the definition of a lost cause. I am irrevocably wicked because just now I opened the door out of a selfish desire to see you again. I wanted to kiss you again. I wanted to close my eyes and... Because I care more about my own broken heart than..." Her fingers flew up to her lips as her eyes filled with tears. "See? I'm a mess!"

He kissed her but this time, it wasn't about heat and fire or the wanton power of the woman in his arms. This time it was about the tenderest taste, the softest and gentlest touch of his mouth to hers, as if he could heal the pain in her eyes and bridge the gulf between them with this kiss alone—by taking nothing and giving her a touch that was reverent and worshipful. He kissed her because he loved her.

"Most gorgeous mess I have ever seen," he whispered. "Come on, Lilly. Tell me again. Here, sit down with me and let's just talk. What you said last night. Was that an attempt to scare me off?"

Lilly nodded solemnly. "Why aren't you scared, Jackson? A Temptress tells you that you're on the short-list for Take Downs and that Upper Management has you flagged for destruction and you are sitting on the edge of my bed and holding my hand. How does that leap happen?"

He hesitated before answering. "I guess you're not very scary, Lilly."

She sat up a little straighter. "You don't believe me, do you?"

"Which part?" he asked cautiously.

Lillith's gaze narrowed. "Different tactic. Which part did you buy?"

"The part where you said you had a lot of baggage," he admitted quietly. "The rest is sort of filed under 'potential female eccentric beliefs I'm going to ignore until she starts putting pentagrams on our Christmas tree and then we'll negotiate a compromise".

Her mouth fell open. "Are you serious?"

"Dead serious."

"Damn," she whispered. "Perfection has its flaws after all. I know love blinds because I think once I saw you I stopped looking at anything else but you can't endanger yourself with this...blind faith in me."

"I'm not being blind."

"No? Circling back for crazy women is something you do with your eyes wide open?" She tipped her head to one side, sexy in her defiance.

"For dangerous crazy, no. But for interesting crazy, for fun crazy, a man circles back if he has any sense at all. Life is too short to miss out on this brand of crazy, Lilly. I think I was missing this before." Jackson covered her hand with his. "It might have been an uphill journey with some struggles but it was always a straight line. You. You are all curves, Lillith Fields."

"How are you editing the word 'demon' out of this?" she asked.

"I'm trying to ease into that part." Jackson sighed. "Every time you say that word I remember an old picture I saw in a book once with a storm of red-skinned imps yanking up a bunch of medieval farmers up by their heels. But then you said something about an employee ID and departments so now I'm picturing those weird red things punching in their time cards before they start poking people with molten spears."

Lilly shook her head. "First of all, Hell has never held or received a single human soul much less bothered them with a single blister. Souls are not bobble heads to be collected, Jackson. Each soul is a human's own and for better or worse you get to keep it for the long haul."

"What's the long haul?" he asked.

"Not my department. But the red skin maggot look for any employee of Hell is also out! It was never an accurate depiction. We *always* strived to appear human and since 1504, demons were guaranteed to be as attractive as their angelic counterparts."

"1504?"

"Big landmark in the Corporation. It's when we were pulled back to—" She stopped abruptly. "You know what, Jackson? I think I'm off track here. I'm wasting time making some kind of ridiculous educational pitch as if it makes a difference if you believe me, as if pulling the curtain back to let you peek behind the scenes of Hades Enterprises makes this any better."

"It has to! I want to know who you are, Lilly. I want to get past this fantasy smokescreen and—"

"*Get past this?*" she squeaked. "Jackson, I am a *demon.* You are a *human being!*"

"I'm looking right at you, Lilly. You're as human as I am."

"You're so far off base with that statement, I'm waiting for lightning to strike."

Jackson spread his arms out, a willing sacrifice. "Not even a rumble of thunder. I think I'm in the clear. I don't care if you're from another planet, Lilly, unless you're hinting that we're not a physically compatible species to—"

"Oh, we're compatible! And if you'd taken your damn pants off last night, I'd have compatibly taken you to the moon and back—but that's as far as it goes! I am created for the one night stand, Jackson, and—*You*! You ruined me!" Lilly's furious pout was a glorious thing to behold and Jackson struggled to ignore the effects on his body.

"That's a first. A woman is ruined because we omitted the hit-and-run."

She punched him in the upper arm but not hard enough to hurt him. "I need to keep you safe, Jackson. I need you to trust me. Kiss me one more time and then run. Run as if all the Hounds of Hell are on your heels, because they might be. Okay?"

"Nope." He recaptured her hands with his, tenderly trying to hold her still. "I'll kiss you as many times as I can manage but I've decided not to run."

She abruptly pulled her hands from his and stood from the bed. "You running is non-negotiable. You promised to leave by ten and if you refuse to sprint when the time comes, then maybe I need to start moving you toward the door now."

"Lilly, slow down." He stood up to try to calm her but also to keep her close just in case things spiraled in a new weird direction. "You're talking about my safety. Tell me exactly what the danger is and let me see if I can help."

"Oh, Hell, no! I'm not describing the Big Ugly so that you can nod and smile and add it to your mental file of "small talk topics to avoid with my new girlfriend"!"

He could see that she was angry with him but the word 'girlfriend' triggered a happy maelstrom somewhere inside of him. He forced himself to focus on the present and not the fantasies of what life held in the weeks, months and years ahead with Lilly at his side. "Okay, you don't want to talk about it but surely you can see where I'm struggling to take in the need for a Casablanca kiss without knowing about the Nazis."

She blinked at him. "Good movie."

"It's a classic." Jackson started to smile. This was the world's most ridiculous conversation and he couldn't care less. "Since sports metaphors are off the table, I thought I'd change it up."

"Jackson, you need to go."

"I have eight minutes. Take your coat off and stay a while, Lilly."

"We have eight minutes. Take off your clothes and give me something to remember you by before you go," she countered dryly, a temptress struggling for some dignity in the midst of defeat. "No? Okay. The plane's leaving, Rick. I'll tell the Nazis you said hello."

Jackson crossed his arms. "Rick wasn't the one to get on the plane in Casablanca. Good guys stay. I'm staying."

"I stand corrected. I'm the one who should have run and I've stayed too long already. Last night, when I got the summons I…just wanted to steal a few more hours of freedom. I unplugged the hotel phone. I took a bubble bath, packed my bags and I cried. I repeated your name until I couldn't say it anymore and that felt like victory. But it was a mistake. I should have gone. This is selfish to look at you, to linger like a spoiled child who knows the park is about to close."

"You unplugged the phone? Well that explains why you weren't picking up."

"You tried to call me?"

"Enough times to qualify for a restraining order."

She beamed at him. "Thank you, Jackson."

"Lilly. You have all the power. Forget the clock. Kiss me again and let's put this Temptress thing in perspective. I've got 'Casablanca' on my laptop. We can order in room service and hide out for as long as it takes." Jackson pulled her into his arms. "What do you say?"

"I don't have a say." She shook her head slowly. "I was summoned."

"Like a court order?"

She pushed against him and he gently released her. "I. Was. *Summoned*."

Jackson swallowed hard. The word suddenly had more weight and he felt a small tendril of ice start to uncurl down his spine. "Summoned by whom?"

"My manager," she said softly. "No demon can ignore or defy a summons when it is…binding. Asmodeus is one of the Ancients so trust me, the guy knows how to phrase his orders to avoid any messy loopholes."

"Asmodeus. Why do I vaguely know that name?"

"Babylonian God demoted to a princely title in Hell if you believe Dante. All I know is that once an entity has enjoyed having temples built to them and dancing virgins it's hard to get excited about quarterly employee performance reports or fresh donuts in the break room."

"I have the weirdest impulse to laugh and cry at the same time, Lilly. Your boss cannot possibly be—"

A strange knock on the door reverberated through his chest and a strange flash of light transformed the room to rob it of color. In a blink, it was as if he were standing in a three dimensional rendering of a black and white film. Lilly was in color. He looked down at his shirt and saw blue stripes. It was a surreal sensation that robbed him of speech.

And then there was someone else in the room and he was robbed of a hell of a lot more.

"You are early, Dread Lord!" Lillith stepped back, lifting her hands defensively. "I have a few more minutes."

"I am on time. Tell me that you are not relying on a digital device manufactured six years ago as an accurate time piece and that you aren't about to argue with an Immortal Prince about his punctuality!" Asmodeus was in no mood for her and then froze as he realized that a mortal was in his presence. The curse he mumbled under his breath was so foul, he winced to hear the bathroom mirror shatter.

The human, on the other hand, didn't flinch. He stared at Asmodeus, shaken but calm enough to hold out his arm toward Lillith. "Lilly, come here, behind me, baby."

Lilly's sweet expression of shock was telling. "J-Jackson. That is very brave of you but I think you might be wiser to stand behind me."

Asmodeus glared at her. "What have you told him?!"

"Nothing." She lifted her chin one defiant inch with the lie and did her best to pull it off. But Asmodeus' glare was acid enough to burn the skin off of a tank and she faltered. She cleared her throat and decided to attempt to add an amendment. "Well, I may have slipped him a few details regarding my mission but he doesn't believe a word of it. Or…he didn't…until you…just materialized in my hotel room in front of him."

"I'm right here, Lilly. Let's not make me doubt my sanity more than I already do by speaking about me in the third person, okay?"

Lilly spared him an apologetic glance. "Sorry, Jackson."

"Mr. Kent," Asmodeus addressed him directly in a voice so calm it was terrifying. "You should return to your party downstairs and to your life. I understand that your event was a vast success and that even now your assistant is searching for you to tell you about a new legitimate last-minute donation that will surpass all your fund-raising goals. Every dream you had for that small hospital is achieved and more. Congratulations, sir."

Jackson moved but only to step in front of Lilly.

The hotel room door re-opened with a wave of Asmodeus's well-manicured hand. "It was a pleasure meeting you. Good-bye."

"Good-bye. Lilly, tell your boss to have a nice trip and let's wish him all the best in his—um, future endeavors." Jackson reached back and drew her tighter against his back. "Feel free to walk through that door, guy, or go poof, but the only one leaving this room is you."

Lilly wasn't sure what to feel. She was awash in fear but also renewed love and pride for the way her fragile mortal Jackson thought he was going to command a god, save the damsel and win the day.

Asmodeus smiled. "Your attachment to the Temptress is not unique. Many of her previous targets have mistaken their desire and lust for something else and proclaimed their undying love as they spent themselves inside of her. But your affections will fade quickly, mortal."

Oh, shit. Here it comes.

"Temptress, kneel."

Lillith slipped from Jackson's hold and immediately knelt at Asmodeus feet, her head bowed in submission. Her will was forfeit and even as her heart broke, it was rage she felt the most. Freedom was denied to her. Demons were not given choices and did not have the gift of free will. She was powerless. Obedience was the meter of existence…and defiance its end.

"Lilly, no!" Jackson started to touch her shoulder but she was as cold as stone—and just as immovable.

"She is mine to command, Mr. Kent. Mine."

"You're wrong, Ace." Jackson put up his hands. "You don't get to own anyone."

Asmodeus shook his head with a sigh. "What do you see kneeling there, Mr. Kent? Is she all that you would wish for? She who has gleefully parted her thighs for more men than there are leaves on an oak tree? She who knows no remorse, no guilt, no conscience? She has achieved a king's ecstasy and then casually watched him die moments later on the battlefield. She has trailed the hem of her skirts in plague-ridden streets to expose perverted bishops and attended more public executions than you've scored points on a board. In fact, I think she took the same sort of glee in her victories that you take in yours. What do you see now, Mr. Kent? Isn't she lovely?"

"She…is the most beautiful thing I have ever seen." Jackson defiance was so pure that Lilly began to weep.

Asmodeus' smiles vanished. "Abase yourself, Temptress and tell Mr. Kent farewell."

Tears flowed down her cheeks but Lilly shifted to kiss Jackson's shoes. "J-Jackson. Go. P-please."

"Lilly, stop!" Jackson knelt down instantly, his voice rough with emotion. "This cannot be happening!"

Asmodeus was unmoved by the scene. "Release the whore."

At the word 'whore', Lilly simply knew. *Oh, here we go.*

Jackson's tackle came so fast and without warning that Asmodeus was slammed into the wall before it registered that things had gone too far. Lilly's scream was genuine as chaos unlike any the cosmos had seen unfolded. Asmodeus, a Prince of Hell, Immortal of the First Circle and former demi-god, was on his ass and his nose broken by a human being whose only advantage in that moment was surprise and rage.

But surprise is over in the blink of an eye and with it went Jackson's advantage.

Lilly screamed again, finding her feet to put herself in between them, cursing the indulgence of the coat for making her clumsier but grateful for the padding as she absorbed the worst of her supervisor's physical blows. The pain was unspeakable but Lillith was unfazed. She was an imperfect shield but a stubborn one. Instead of trying to fend Asmodeus off, she recklessly clung to him by viciously gripping his ears and wrapping her legs around his waist.

"Run, Jackson! Run!"

Jackson was not cooperating by running. He was fighting his way to his feet and she could see in his eyes a warrior gathering his strength for the battle. He wasn't thinking about his odds of survival. He wasn't thinking at all.

He was going to save the woman he loved.

And then the world went black and for Lilly there was only one last silent plea to Upper Management to spare Jackson Kent from death.

Chapter Fourteen

Jackson opened his eyes.

He was instantly mentally alert.

Hospital? Mental ward? Morgue? Where'd we land?

He sat up quickly and regretted it. It was hard to get oriented and a wave of dizzy nausea caught him by the throat but he fought past it.

Lilly needs me so mount up cowboy.

It was hard to get oriented because the room was black. Black polished floors, black carved stone walls, black folding screens and ornately worked columns and not a window anywhere. Light came from one candelabra of lit black tapers set on a desk that looked as if it were made from a single piece of onyx. Jackson frowned as he ran his hand over the black leather fainting couch he'd been lying on. Other than the desk, it was the only piece of furniture in the room.

"What the hell?" he muttered.

"You are an astute man," a voice replied and a handsome gentleman in a black tailored suit came out behind one of the screens with a silver tray tea set. "Darjeeling? I know you're not generally a tea in the afternoon sort of person, but since the setting is already strange, why not try something soothing and yet vaguely familiar?"

"Where is Lillith? Where am I? Who are you? Are you supposed to be Satan or something like that?" Jackson stood up and simply ignored the disorientation the maneuver set off. "And where is Asmodeus? I need to kill him."

The man merely raised his eyebrows at the threat and then smiled. "That was the definition of a barrage of questions, my dear sir. I hope you don't mind if I cherry pick the easy ones first."

"It's your show."

"You are in my private apartments. I am Malcolm and I am not Lucifer, though I appreciate the nod. Currently, I am the acting Regent of Hades Enterprises, Limited Liability Corporation or Hell as it's more commonly known. It's a temporary position for me if Upper Management is merciful but we are short a Lucifer at the moment. The position should be filled soon and then I will cheerfully go back to being the Prince of Darkness's Executive Personal Assistant. In the meantime, here we are." He set the tray down on the desk, the candlelight illuminating the silver and his features more clearly. He straightened and gestured for Jackson to come closer. "Why don't you join me?"

Jackson walked over refusing to look intimidated. "Don't take this the wrong way, but I am really not interested in the niceties. I appreciate the effort to make me feel…comfortable, but if this is really Hell, isn't that counter to the mission statement?"

"Not at all!" Malcolm looked cheerfully affronted. "I am proud to say that if I know anything about anything it's comfort. And whenever the *extremely* rare chance comes to be hospitable to a human guest, I think I knock it out of the park. Would you prefer wine? I have an excellent red wine from a small Napa winery that the last Lucifer discovered. Very smooth and not too heavy for this early in the day in my humble opinion."

Jackson blinked. He wanted to ask what happened to the last Lucifer, but he was afraid that once he was completely off topic there'd be no going back. Besides, if he realized that even a small part of him believed that he was actually in Hell, he wasn't sure he wouldn't end up in a rubber room.

God help me. I might already be in a rubber room except... Lilly needs me. Deep breath. Pull it together.

"Great. Wine. Please tell me where Lilly is."

"Lilly." Malcolm sighed and uncorked the bottle of red wine that had mysteriously replaced the tea set and began to fill two crystal goblets. "Lillith is safe at the moment. I intervened and she is being held until a decision can be reached."

Jackson's chest tightened with icy fear. "A decision involving what exactly?"

Malcolm held out the goblet. "A decision about what comes next."

Jackson took the glass without tasting the wine, politely going through the motions while his brain reeled. "She did nothing wrong."

"I'm inclined to agree." Malcolm took a sip of his wine and closed his eyes to savor it. "Damn, I miss him."

"Pardon?"

Malcolm's eyes opened instantly as if he were recalling that he had company. "Sorry. Nostalgia for a friend. But come, I'm going to insist that we sit down together. I'll answer any questions you have and we will find a solution to this conundrum together. Deal?"

Jackson's brow furrowed. "Who are you again?"

"Just a Regent, Mr. Kent. No deals with the Devil are on the table today."

"Any questions I have?"

"No limits and almost nothing in reserve." Malcolm leaned with a confidential wink. "I am a Company Man so you'll have to give me a little wiggle room, Mr. Kent."

"Okay. I'll sit."

Malcolm led him into another black room shaped like an octagon with an octagon table at its center. Overhead, a black candlelit crystal chandelier was suspended by no chains that Jackson could discern and reflected off every polished surface giving the overall impression that they the room was suspended in space and time.

Jackson tentatively took a seat and shook his head. "I'm going to ask my mom to crochet some doilies or placemats to break this up for you, Malcolm."

Malcolm grinned as he took the chair nearest Jackson. "I would be honored."

"Malcolm. Why am I in Hell?"

"Because I don't have the security codes to get you into the offices of Heaven, Inc. and this seemed like the best place to catch our breath." Malcolm took a small sip of his wine. "If you don't mind, I would like to start things off by apologizing."

"Apologizing for what?"

"Well, it's a long list but let's grapple the big items first. Upper Management has a policy against issuing apologies but I'll express this one on a personal basis. I'm truly sorry for all the trouble we've caused you. I found out early on about the misfire but was under strict orders not to share it, even with the Temptations Department itself. You see, normally when a person is flagged for a take down, they've earned it. The worst mortals you can imagine have been historically flagged and even then it's only when they are such skilled liars and deceivers that no human beings around them are aware of just how repugnant they are. It's a subtle kind of search and destroy and Upper Management doesn't use it too often."

"So, I'm one of the worst?" Jackson asked solemnly. "I mean…I'm obviously not now but was I fated to go crazy and commit mass murder or something? Was that why—Lilly was sent to…seduce me? To stop me?"

"I like you, Jackson Kent. You aren't sputtering over there in outrage and defensively listing all your good deeds. Amazing, but let's just end the suppositions that are going to rob you of some great sleep." Malcolm put his glass down. "You are a good man, sir. In fact, you are what some religions would deem a 'righteous man'. Feel better?"

"Nope."

"The mission was a red herring. Apparently, Upper Management was demonstrating its prerogative to do whatever it wants and they do enjoy the ancient ritual of a test. I think the most famous record I can compare it to is Job. Poor man!"

"Job?"

"Sure. Righteous man. Big Test. Endless fodder for sermons and may I say more than one debate about why it's still in Management's playbook considering that that wasn't exactly a great story. Good prose but a wretched story if you stand back and look at it." Malcolm retrieved his glass. "You aren't drinking your wine."

"I'm…not thirsty."

"One taste. It feels rude to drink pure paradise in front of you."

Jackson dutifully took a sip and set the goblet down once and for all. "It's great," he offered without much enthusiasm. "Okay, I just got 'tested' for whatever reason and I'm guessing I passed somehow or I'd be sitting with my feet in boiling oil or brimstone or whatever you're using these days, right?"

"You passed and I'm going to ignore that jab about brimstone."

"Lilly said something about failure. She was terrified about being summoned and then," Jackson paused to pause and take a deep breath to keep his cool, "And then that Asmodeus guy showed up and he *hit* her! Listen up, Malcolm. I don't honestly give a shit what passes in your rule book but in mine, you never, *ever* hit a woman. He—if you don't fire his ass, then by all means, put him in a room with me and I'll deal with him!"

Malcolm looked at him as if in awe. "Wow. I… You have left me speechless, sir."

"He. Hit. Her." Jackson's hands fisted helplessly against his thighs. "How about flagging that?!"

"Yes." Malcolm put his hands up in surrender. "In the review, it was admitted that you attacked him first and that he only struck Lillith in an effort to break *your* neck in retaliation. An impulsive choice for which he has profusely apologized and he is now facing the strictest Sanctions of both Heaven and Hell. He is in—how can I phrase this? Asmodeus is in a Cosmic Time Out. He has been sent to a very humiliating corner to sit with his nose against the wall and there is some discussion of his potential demotion to playing receptionist in our lobby for a few centuries. I know it's not the scaffold or the guillotine you were hoping for, but trust me, humiliation for a demi-god is way worse than an end to existence! They'd rather blink into the void than become a topic for office gossip."

Jackson's rage was deflated a few degrees as he pictured the big, pretty brute he'd met sitting on a tiny stool in a corner like a three year old who'd painted on the walls. "He insulted Lilly. But I…probably could have handled it better as well."

"You broke his nose!" Malcolm said it as if Jackson had performed an incredible feat.

"I was going for shock and awe so he'd let Lilly go," Jackson confessed, hating the guilt that lashed through him. "He deserved it!"

"Shock and awe, indeed!" Malcolm whistled. "Well, that little snippet will provide viral entertainment for the employees of Hades for centuries to come!"

"Great. I'll cross it off my bucket list."

"Oh, did you have breaking a Babylonian God's nose on your bucket list? Because if so I will pay you handsomely for a copy of that piece of paper!" Malcolm joked, then sobered just as quickly when he saw that Jackson was not joining in the fun. "Sorry."

"What about Lilly?"

"Mr. Kent—"

"If you people are holding her to punish or hurt her for some imaginary failure, then that shit ends right here. She did *nothing* wrong and if her mission was about seducing me and changing my life, then she was gloriously successful. The pants may not have come off but that's a technicality! She was kind and caring and funny and…she's perfect. She is perfect."

Jackson wasn't sure how it happened but the jovial charming man in front of him suddenly became a very still and strong presence, all business and all power—and he did it without the flicker of a single lash.

"Here is the dilemma. Lillith is a demon. She was not born, Mr. Kent. She was created and crafted to be one thing—a Temptress and not just any Temptress, but the best of the best. She is forged in heat and sexual fires; completely attuned to appetite, to hunger and to an awareness of every way the human brain can fire and every way you seek pleasure. But there are things she was never meant to master."

Jackson swallowed, a captive audience of one, anxious to hear every word but also terrified that the time for posturing and banter was gone. "Go on."

"She was never meant to feel tenderness, to lose her bearings, to demonstrate a conscience of any kind." Malcolm tapped his glass and watched it magically refill. "Demons can perform good and bad deeds as we are commanded but going 'soft'—it is a special kind of danger for us."

Us. Sure. Why did I miss that?

"Why dangerous?" Jackson asked.

"Because it gets in the way of fulfilling our duties and we are not permitted to fail to do our duties." Malcolm folded his hands together on the table. "The hierarchy is not kind when an employee falls out of step. It has been proposed that a quick end is more merciful than the torture of an eternity of living with bitter failure and the retribution of unforgiving demonic peers. As I said, some creatures prefer a blink into the void over the alternative."

"What are you saying?"

"I'm saying that Upper Management is watching this one closely but has refused to voice an edict to tell me what to do with a Temptress who fails to destroy a man who didn't deserve to be destroyed then preemptively takes out another man who probably deserved to be flagged but wasn't. She is a Temptress who violated every secrecy protocol I can think of by telling you about the Corporation and then topped off a historical list of violations by assaulting a superior entity in defense of a human being and thereby saving the life of the aforementioned 'righteous man'. I'm in a bind, Mr. Kent."

"No bind. I'm not telling anyone about this because I don't want to end up in a rubber room and as far as I can see, any leader has to look at the results, not just the steps to get there. Right? No harm, no foul, Malcolm."

"The harm is that Lillith is made useless by these events. She cannot be trusted in the field again and there is serious concern that her abilities are compromised beyond recovery. She desires none but you, Mr. Kent. I'll pause for a moment just so that we can both soak in the disastrous implications."

Malcolm took a slow measured sip from his glass as reverently as a priest taking communion and then waited for Jackson's head to catch up with his heart.

"She desires none but me," Jackson repeated the words reverently. "Wow…"

"No. Not wow!" Malcolm chided. "I mean, yes, of course, that's a level of insane devotion that might warrant a 'wow' or two, but you're missing the main thrust of my speech, Mr. Kent. A Temptress who has gone soft will not survive in Hades. Even if I spare her, they will tear her to pieces the first time she strays into the halls to get a croissant from the employee break room. I'm afraid it's a bit like bees smelling fear."

"That's a myth. Bees can't smell fear."

"Really? You're going to argue myths with a Demon of the First Plane?" Malcolm crossed his arms. "You are deliberately being obtuse to avoid facing the truth about Lillith."

Jackson's heart began to pound so hard he couldn't believe that it wasn't audible to the Regent of Hell. "She's doomed. Is that what you're politely saying over there as you sip red wine and sigh about how tough it is at the top?"

"We are what we are. We are demons. It is not in our nature to change, Mr. Kent."

Doomed. She won't survive in Hades. We are what we are.

It hit Jackson like lightning. The answer like a narrow golden thread of hope that might just be strong enough to unravel the whole tangled mess he'd made.

"Because you don't get the hiccups."

"Pardon?" Malcolm's left eyebrow arched in an expression of surprise. "Yes. Come to think of it, we do not get the hiccups."

"And you don't cry."

"We do *not*."

"And you don't fall in love."

Malcolm's eyes darkened with a sad, mournful echo of thoughts he would never give voice. "No. We do not love. Not like you do."

"Then Lilly isn't a demon. Not anymore."

"What?"

"Lilly isn't a demon anymore because she does all those things! Because it is in her nature to change, to break the rules, and to love me. To love me enough to let me keep my pants on, to let me hit her with a snowball and…she changed! Lilly cried and Asmodeus saw it! You ask old Ace if he made her cry and then you're not just hearing it from me. *Lillith is not a demon!*" Jackson stood up, a man on fire with the blaze of his triumph. "Let her go."

Malcolm also stood, slowly in shock. "I'm not sure it's possible what you're suggesting. Well-meant and very sweet but—"

A phone rang in the other room where his desk was and Malcolm strode out without looking back, aware that Jackson was right on his heels.

Malcolm picked up the receiver and Jackson was treated to a one-sided conversation unlike any other.

"Yes. Can we confirm the tears? Yes. No, Lord of Light. No. He said 'hiccups'. I would never jest about such a thing. No. It is completely unprecedented. I understand." Malcolm lowered his head and closed his eyes. "On my head be it. I make the formal request and accept all consequences."

Malcolm put the phone down and ended the call, his expression wary and cautious. "Mr. Kent? Can you answer one more question for me?"

"Yes."

"Do you love her still? Knowing what you know? Knowing her true nature? Knowing—that there is a universe about her that you will never know? Is that truly possible?"

Jackson held his breath and he sensed it. His life and hers hung in the balance and it was this answer that was going to decide it all.

Chapter Fifteen

Lilly had been commanded to pack every article of clothing she possessed for an "extended mission". Every folded item was added to her luggage with a heavy heart. They had not offered any details of her destination, so she included her new winter gear with dread. Fur and cashmere was all well and good but if they vindictively sent her to Siberia, she wouldn't be surprised so it was better to be prepared for anything.

Her phone rang and she smiled to see Benjamin's code.

"Ben. Are they burning me in effigy yet?"

Ben's awkward laugh was telling. "No. Not yet, Lill."

"Oh, well. Give it time. Any whispers about where they're shipping me to?"

Ben sighed. "No. No one's talking and I don't have any mission designated for you in the system. The records are blank. I'm…worried about you."

"Did you find him?" she whispered. "Is he safe?"

"I found him. Here, I'll look again." The sound of Ben's keyboard coming to life underlined his reply. "He checked out of the hotel and from what I can see from airline records, went home to his apartment. More telling, Lilly, there's a binding protection order signed off by the Corporation. He's more than safe."

The relief that poured through her was so powerful she had to sit down. "Okay. Nothing else matters. I told him to run and he must have listened. I blacked out and— never mind. Time to face my punishment."

"Lilly…"

"I don't think I'm coming back, Ben. I'm packing like a kid going off to college but I think it's all for show. I—blew it."

"Don't kid yourself. There's not a college kid on the planet who can compete with your wardrobe."

Lillith let out a long slow breath. "I want to thank you, Ben. For everything. You're a good demon, Ben."

"Thanks, Lillith." He didn't bother to deny the worst. "I'm going to miss you around here."

"Try to partner with Jezebel. That girl will keep you on your toes for centuries."

"She doesn't have your sense of humor."

"No one does." Lillith rolled her eyes. "Probably for the best. Good-bye, Benjamin."

"Good-bye."

She disconnected before the lump in her throat made her feel like more of a fool. She was a useless demon until she recovered her old self but Lillith had no desire to return to her former glory. But they hadn't asked what she wanted and she had no choices left. She was broken but defiant, a notoriously unhealthy combination for a Temptress about to head out into the field.

The small mountain of luggage was ready and she smugly eyed her haul.

If they meant to destroy her, she was ready. A slow, tortuous end or a quick blink, it was all the same to her. The man she loved was safe and she was going to go out in style. It was as close to a fairy tale ending as a broken Temptress could hope for—even if she had missed out on getting to take Jackson Kent into her bed.

Shake it off.

If they were sending her back into the game, she would need her wits.

If they were sending her into the void to end her existence with her packed bags just as a humiliating touch, then she would still need her wits. Lillith was determined to keep her chin held high and cling to whatever pride she had left.

She called transport to let them know that she was ready and that her bags were prepared to follow her. The acknowledgement was courteous but icy and it made her sigh.

Wherever I'm going.

The walk from her apartments to the motor pool was strange and more terrifying than she'd expected. Her high heels made a firm staccato rhythm of feigned confidence across the floors and Lilly pasted a look of disdain on her face even as a surreal nightmare surfaced. Because if Hell was anything, it was busy. She should have been navigating through a stream of employees and doing her best to ignore their stares and speculative whispers. Instead there was—nothing. The halls and elevator were deserted and not a single voice was audible. Lilly's steps slowed. The silence was total. Not a keyboard click, not the single rattle of a copy machine or whisper.

Outcast. Holy stones, this is…what it's like. I'm—shut out.

Shunned.

Her walk of defiance became a walk of shame.

Lilly's brow furrowed. She'd have rather jogged through a shitstorm than this silence.

She stepped up onto the small platform designed for individual travel and rolled her eyes at the sci-fi sticker of Mr. Spock some clever motor pool demon had put on the wall. A sense of humor was always appreciated but not necessarily the last thing she wanted to see before her destruction.

There was a familiar warmth before the shift and she welcomed it, closing her eyes.

Only to open them when it was clear she'd landed on her feet, very much still in existence.

No destruction? I would have sworn I'd earned it! Oh, well, there's the first big disappointment of the day.

Nausea gripped her but she waited for it to pass. She was obviously back in the field and expected to demonstrate her loyalty. Lillith found herself standing in the hallway of what was either a luxury hotel or a high-end apartment building. The solid brushed steel door had a brass plate on it with "14A" on it and the carpet runner underneath her feet was new. The lighting was also brushed steel but elegant enough to fend off an industrial appearance. In any case, it all bespoke money and success. Whoever was behind the door to 14A, they'd done well for themselves.

It's a test. A big ugly test of some kind. They're dropping me into the field blind to see if I can still hit it out of the park.

Damn.

Oh, well. I think I would have been happier in Siberia...

Lilly checked her phone. Like the stroll through the company, it was eerily familiar and yet now void. There was no data. No signs of the usual report on the Take Down ahead. No information of any kind on her next target or the main thrust of her new mission.

On the bright side, it looks like I've got great cell reception.

Lillith searched for a few more seconds, tried to contact IT and accepted that there wasn't going to be any help coming from the home office. She was on her own for the first time in her existence.

Unfortunately, the realization brought on the tears she'd been holding back since she put on her best perfume that morning but she fiercely wiped them away with the heel of her hand.

This is very bad. I don't want to make it. I just want...Jackson.

I want what I cannot have.

Okay. No tears. I'll cry later. Later. Shower. Good cover for the bawl of the century. Now it's go time. Curtain up. I know the show. I've played this part a million times. I don't need a prompter from some demonic keyboard jockey.

"Oh, well. Woman up, Temptress," she said through gritted teeth. She shook her shoulders and flipped her hair. "You're the demon for the job. Evil human needs someone to take him down and you can mourn in your cocktail glass later. Time to show Upper Management that you can take any punishment they've come up with."

She forced a smile to her lips. "Time to bring the pain."

Lillith pressed the buzzer and exhaled. It was one of her personal beliefs that it was always better to make first eye contact on an exhale. It was also one of her personal beliefs that a Temptress should never be in the field unprepared, but today was a new day.

At the sound of the door being unlocked, it all fell into place. She summoned every ounce of sexual energy she could muster and composed a stupid thought about being lost in the building, her cell phone not working and needing to use Mr. Mystery's phone to call for a car.

And then the door opened.

"Lillith?"

She didn't answer him at first. She just stared and waited for her heart to start beating again. Because Jackson Kent had never looked so impossibly good and she didn't know how a Temptress could survive the fierce joy that held her in its thrall.

"Lillith." Jackson took her hand and pulled her inside and into his arms. "Welcome home, baby."

"I'm...lost." Lillith tipped her head back, wincing that the lies she'd composed were the first and only thoughts in her mind but also that the lies seemed ironically true. "M-my phone isn't working and...I'm...so lost, Jackson. How is this possible? Are you...really here?"

"It's possible. You're here. I love you, Lilly."

She pushed away from him, hating the mess of tears and hiccups threatening to overtake a very beautiful reunion, but she was struggling to process it all. Happiness was as uncommon as a lottery win in her world but Jackson Kent was looking at her as if he was ready to take a lifetime of impossibilities in stride. "Wait, Jackson. It's a test. Or worse! They're torturing me. They're going to let me see you and believe—and then I'll get shipped off to some brothel near a mining camp and…I think I'm going to throw up."

"Do demons throw up?" he asked cautiously.

"No. Not usually."

"Okay. We're still on track here. Lilly, look at me. You are here. Everything is going to be okay."

"I need to sit down."

He led her inside, practically carrying her into the living room of his beautiful apartment. The view of the city's lights and some kind of park was a blur to her before she landed gently in the middle of his couch. A fire was blazing in a corner fireplace and there was a soft rainbow afghan across the back of a nearby chair, no doubt of his mother's creation.

He knelt at her feet, cradling her hands in his and looking up anxiously into her face. "Just take slow, even breaths."

"I should tell you again before they pull the rug out from under me that I love you, too. It might be my last chance."

Jackson smiled. "They let you go, Lilly."

"Who let me go?" she asked.

"*Them.*" He cleared his throat. "I spoke to Malcolm and we—came to a compromise."

"A compromise," she echoed then shook her head. "With the Regent of Hell? No, Jackson. There is no letting go. There is no negotiation. I'm pretty sure that never in the history of history has any demon ever gotten so much as a—"

Jackson slid a folded sheet of paper out of his back pocket and the goldenrod color of it made her gasp.

"Lillith, it was explained to me that *this* is what is known as an Underwood." He held out the Corporate memo to her, the embossed letterhead gleaming when he unfolded it. "I told Malcolm you were going to need some kind of proof to save me a decade of calming a very paranoid and anxious Temptress before you'd accept what's on the table."

She took the paper from him with numb fingers. "You really spoke to *Malcolm*?"

"I did, although I won't lie to you, Lilly…"

"Sure," she whispered fighting shock. "Let's have it."

"He's a good guy but he's got the decorating tastes of a blind man. I'm going to have mom knit him one of her afghan throws for Christmas. You think he'll be offended?"

Lilly shook her head very slowly. "I'm pretty sure he'll…that'll be a first, Jackson. But you should probably make sure your mother realizes that she has just knitted a blanket for the current temporary overseer of Hell. You know. Just in case she'd rather not."

Jackson smiled. "Nope. I'll just tell her for it's a new friend who's never had a Christmas gift and who is in desperate need of some color in his life and that'll do it."

"Why? *Why* would you do that?" she asked.

"I'd say a baby-soft sample of my mom's knitting is minimal payback for what you have in your hands, wouldn't you?"

Lillith unfolded the memo and read it as slowly as she could.

Her hands shook but the words were unmistakable and Upper Management's font was singular enough to make sure she knew of the document's authenticity.

"Demonic Temptress is hereby released of service from H.E.LLc and shall henceforth be a free agent to please herself and to determine her own path. Previous Non-Disclosure Agreements are still valid and the Temptress will not reveal her nature to anyone other than Jackson Kent, Human Being, who has already been apprised and awarded special status. Hades Enterprises, LLc shall not be held liable for any of her future actions though there is some vast hope that she will do her Company proud as she secretly represents her entire Species amidst the human race. Back pay has been distributed to an account to allow above-mentioned Temptress plenty of resources to avoid any inclinations toward unsavory temptations of her own. She is given into the care of a Jackson Kent, Human Being, for his natural lifetime but if the Demonic Temptress wishes to leave him, she is free to do so.

She is henceforth Unbound and beyond the Sanctions of her former Employer."

"I am Unbound."

"Apparently so." Jackson shifted on his feet nervously. "You're not smiling."

"I'm still taking it all in." Lilly blinked hard and then looked up. "How?"

"I told him that if they wouldn't let you go, then Hades Enterprises, LLc would have its first human in permanent residence because I wasn't leaving without you." Jackson shifted up to sit next to her on the sofa. "I offered to work in the mail room but apparently Hell isn't currently hiring."

"And what was your plan if he'd taken you up on that offer?"

"I was going to make the best of it and pray that I could stay close enough at hand to keep you safe." Jackson shrugged his shoulders and sighed. "I guess he didn't want me breaking any more noses or brawling in the cafeteria, so Malcolm made a phone call and—the rest is a bit of a blur. He released you into my care and said he wished us every happiness and…"

"And?" she asked.

"He may have hinted that you have a weakness for bubble baths and advised me to stock up." Jackson grinned. "I bought out three department stores for high-end bubbles, Lillith."

"You did?"

He nodded. "I love you and if my beautiful Temptress likes bubbles, I'm not the idiot who is going to get in her way."

"You love me." Lillith felt the tension and fear finally unwind from her chest. "I am not exactly lovable, Jackson."

"I love *you*. You are kind and impulsive, funny and sweet. I think you are strong and smart and a force of nature. A man could never get bored discovering all the things you are, Lillith. I want to spend the rest of my life loving you. I want whatever that memo offers for a chance at happiness because without you, I have no chance." Jackson's hold tightened on her hands. "But I want to make it clear that if it's not your choice to stay with me…"

Lilly sat up straighter as realization hit her. "Do you understand that they didn't make me human?"

Jackson's expression saddened but he shook it off. "I asked but Malcolm said that it was not on the table. As for what that really means to have a Temptress out on permanent leave, he didn't know. Babies? Life span? Nobody was willing to give out answers and I didn't want to push too hard because I was afraid they'd rethink it and change their minds. Does it matter? I mean, you're still you. You're just here and apparently unemployed."

"I don't care. I just want you. The rest—the rest of it, we'll make up as we go along, okay?" Lilly's heart was beating faster and faster. "This is really surreal because demons never faint but I swear the room is spinning."

"Never?"

Lilly punched him in the shoulder. "Never."

"You are free. Free to do whatever you want but oh, man, I am praying that what you'll want to do is stay, Lilly. Stay with me."

"I can't believe it."

He smiled and pulled her into his arms. "It's going to take some time for you to adjust to this, I'm guessing. Living with human beings…with me."

"You want this? You want me? Even knowing what I am?"

"I love you and I know it's been a bit of a blur but I can honestly say that I've been to Hell and back to win you, Lillith Fields. How's that for a start?"

Tears filled her eyes as all the possibilities began to flood her mind. "I think that's the most beautiful thing I've ever heard!"

"Then how does this sound?" Jackson cradled her against him. "Marry me, Lilly."

She blinked in shock. "M-marry? I'm…there's that cliché about milk and cows and I feel like I should explain to you that you've won a dairy farm, Jackson. I don't think I'm—qualified to wear white, Jackson."

"Lillith," Jackson sighed. "Don't take this the wrong way but it would serve them all right if we refused to live in sin. Don't you think?" He gifted her with a mischievous smile all his own. "We could invite Malcolm to the wedding if you want."

She nodded slowly, her joy so bright and fierce and hot she was afraid it would choke her. "Let's ask him to give me away!"

"So, that's a yes?"

"Yes, yes, yes! And oh, man! It's going to be one Hell of a Reception, Mr. Jackson Kent!"

He laughed and kissed her until they were both breathless.

"Let's hope so, Lilly! Let's hope so!"

Author Notes:

Jackson Kent was originally conceived as a professional quarterback in the NFL. I've had a vicarious love affair with the sport for most of my life but recent events ended that. I just couldn't glorify a fictional player when night after night the realities of the National Football League eroded my belief that if I were looking for a "righteous man" who could survive long term, he wouldn't be a product of that environment, culture or system. No hate mail, please. But then I decided that if I can write fiction, then I can write an ideal that I desperately want to see reflected in the real world.

So Jackson Kent got to keep his jersey.

Also, there is a very real Snow Angels organization that supports colorectal cancer patients by helping them with snow removal services (among other support services) in West Des Moines, Iowa. I borrowed the name with their permission but if you would like to contact the real agency and lend your praise and support to their efforts, I know that they would love to hear it. You can find them online at www.coloncanceriowa.org and on FaceBook at DavidsFight. I should quickly say that I hope they aren't horrified to find their name in the midst of a romantic comedy involving the employees of Hades Enterprises, LLc. But I did ask them first, so again, no hate mail, friends.

And one last apologetic note. I don't ski. The extent of my expertise is that fleeting kind we all get after watching a few minutes of the winter Olympics. (You know, where suddenly you're cheering about someone's technique or those soft edges in the downhill or you're pointing out how that guy needs to bend his knees more…when you yourself cannot walk across an icy sidewalk without doing a very ugly split.) I dream of visiting a luxurious resort in Aspen sometime in June in the future. Please. No hate mail, snow bunnies.

Made in the USA
Las Vegas, NV
28 March 2023

69790141R00066